The Story Of Jessie

by

MABEL QUILLER-COUCH

The story of jessie
by Mabel Quiller-Couch

ISBN: 978-93-63053-52-6

Published by

DOUBLE 9 BOOKS

2/13-B, Ansari Road
Daryaganj, New Delhi – 110002
info@double9books.com
www.double9books.com
Tel. 011-40042856

ABOUT THE AUTHOR

Mabel Quiller-Couch, a prominent figure in early 20th-century literature, penned her masterpiece "The Making Of Mona" as a captivating exploration of human nature and societal norms. Set against the backdrop of the English countryside, Quiller-Couch's novel intricately weaves together themes of love, ambition, and identity, offering readers a nuanced portrayal of life in rural England. In "The Making Of Mona," Quiller-Couch masterfully depicts the journey of the titular character as she navigates the complexities of womanhood and self-discovery. Through richly drawn characters and vivid descriptions of the landscape, Quiller-Couch paints a vivid portrait of rural life and the struggles faced by individuals striving to carve out their own path in a changing world. With its blend of romance, drama, and social commentary, "The Making Of Mona" stands as a testament to Quiller-Couch's literary prowess and her ability to capture the essence of the human experience. Through the lens of Mona's journey, readers are invited to contemplate the nature of identity, ambition, and the pursuit of happiness in a world filled with both opportunity and challenge.

CONTENTS

CHAPTER I
A LETTER FOR SUNNYSIDE COTTAGE

Thomas Dawson was busy in the kitchen trying to make the kettle boil, and to get the fire clear that he might do a piece of toast. He had already tidied up the grate and swept the floor, and as he stood by the table with the loaf in his hand, about to cut a slice, his eye wandered down through the dewy, sunny garden, where every tree and bush was beginning to show a little film of green over its brown branches.

But before he could notice anything in the garden, his attention was attracted by the sight of Daniel Magor, the postman, standing at the gate and fumbling with the latch. Thomas dropped the loaf and the knife, and went out to meet him, leaving the house-door wide open to the beautiful morning sunshine, which poured in in a wide stream right across the kitchen, lighting up with golden radiance the flowers in the window, the old-fashioned photographs on the wall, the china on the dressers, and the cat lying asleep on the scarlet cushion in the arm-chair by the fire.

When he saw Thomas coming the postman ceased fumbling with the latch and waited, holding two letters in his hand.

"Lovely weather, Mr. Dawson. You ain't to work this morning!" he remarked in a tone of surprise.

Thomas shook his head slowly. "No, my wife is bad, she've been bad all night with a sick headache. She's better this morning, but I stayed home to get her some breakfast, and tidy up a bit. When anybody's sick they don't feel they want to do much."

"You'm right," agreed the postman feelingly. "I gets sick headaches very bad myself, and when I wakes with one it seems to me I don't care whether folk gets their letters or not. I am glad I didn't feel like that this morning, Mr. Dawson, for it's good to be alive on such a day, and I've got two letters for you."

"Both of 'em for me!" said Thomas in surprise, and holding out his hand to take them. "I don't think I've had two to once in my life before."

The postman laughed. "If folks didn't get more than you do we postmen would soon be out of a job, I reckon!" But Thomas was gazing at his letters with such a perplexed, preoccupied air, that he did not reply, and Daniel, with a long, inquiring look at him, said "Good-morning," and went on his way.

"One is the seed-list," muttered Thomas to himself, as he retraced his steps through the garden under the budding May-trees, "but it passes my understanding to know who can have sent the other. It—it can't be from—from her," he added, with sudden thought, speaking as though it pained him even to put such a thought into words.

The old cat, hearing his footsteps on the path, roused herself and went out to meet him, but for once he paid no heed to her, and passing into the house sat himself down in the chair by the window, while he still gazed with troubled eyes at the outside of the envelope, and the blurred post-mark which told him nothing. Moments passed before he could summon up courage to open it, for in his heart he felt almost certain who the writer was, and he dreaded to read what might be written; and when at last he did make up his mind, his hand trembled so as he tore open the envelope, that his misty eyes could scarcely make out what was written, or take in the meaning.

"Dear Father and Mother "—for seconds he was unable to read beyond that beginning, so strange yet familiar it seemed after all these years of silence—"I hope you will not refuse to open a letter from me, and I hope that you will try to forgive me for all that's past, and for what I am about to do. You would if you knew all. I wrote to you and told you I had married Harry Lang. I hope you had the letter and read it. I was happy enough for a time, but Harry has had no work to speak of for more than a year, and though we've sold all the little I'd got together, we have been nearly starving many a time. At last, though, Harry has got a good job offered him in a gentleman's racing stables. It is a fine berth to have got, the wages is good, and there are rooms to live in, and we can't refuse it after all we have been through, but they won't allow no children.

"If work hadn't been so hard to get, and we starving, we would have waited for something else, for it nearly kills me to part with my Jessie, but I've got to, and, dear father and mother, I hope you will forgive me, but I am sending her to you. She is all I've got, and I am nearly crazy at losing her, but I don't know what else to do. Life is very hard sometimes. I know you will be good to her, and you can't help loving her, I know. She is very good and quiet, and she will not give mother very much trouble, and I pray with all my heart she may be a better child, and more of a comfort to you than I have ever been.

"Your broken-hearted but loving,

"Lizzie.

"P.S.—She is five years old and strong and healthy. I had her christened Jessamine May to remind me of the jessamine and the May-trees at home, for I love my old home dearer than any place in the world. Forgive me, dear father and mother, and be good to my precious darling."

For minutes after he had reached the end of the letter, poor Thomas Dawson sat with tears running fast over his weather-worn cheeks. "My little maid," he kept saying to himself, with a sob in his breath, "my Lizzie starving! starving! and me with a plenty and to spare!" It was his own child he was thinking of, his own Lizzie, the little maiden who had been the apple of his eye, the joy and pride of his life—and this was what she had come to!

The kettle sang and boiled on the hob, the fire burnt clear, but the loaf lay on the table uncut, and still the old man sat staring before him at the letter spread on the table, heeding nothing until a thought came which roused him completely—though only to a deeper sense of trouble. "However am I going to break the news to mother," he groaned. "Oh, my! but it'll upset her something cruel—and that lazy, good-for-nothing fellow that she could never abide, have brought it all upon us!"

His thoughts and his wonderings, though, were brought to a sudden stop by the touch of a hand on his shoulder. "Why, Thomas, you were so quiet I thought you must be asleep, or ill, or something, and I was so worried I had to get up at last and come down and see." Then, as her husband turned to her, and she caught sight of his face, she grew really alarmed. "What is it? What has happened? There is trouble, I can see it. Tell me what it is, quick, for pity's sake. Don't 'ee keep me waiting."

He rose, and gently putting her into the chair he had been occupying, he handed her Lizzie's letter. "That's the trouble, mother," he said; "it might have been worse—that's all I can say. You must read it for yourself, it'd choke me to do so if I was to try," and he went away to the door and stood there gazing out at the sunny garden where the daffodils bowed gently before the soft breeze, and the crocuses opened their golden cups to the sun.

But he saw nothing, all his mind was given to his wife, and the letter she was reading, and to wondering how she would bear it, and what he could say to comfort her.

At last a long low cry reached him, and he turned hastily back into the kitchen; but, instead of seeing her white and shaken and weeping, as he was prepared to see her, the face that looked up to him was quivering with eagerness and love and joy.

"She's sending us her little one, father!" she gasped in a voice quavering with glad excitement. "Lizzie's little girl, our own little grandchild! We shall have a child about the place again, something to love and work for. You see, Lizzie turns to us in her trouble, poor girl, and it must be a terrible trouble to her," with a momentary sadness dimming the joy in her eyes. "But, oh, I am so thankful, so happy." Then, springing to her feet, "I am well now! this is the medicine I wanted. Father, when do you think she will come? I must get the place all nice and tidy, and a room ready for her, in good time too, and it seems to me I'd best set to work at once or I shall never get a half done!"

Thomas did not say much, his heart was too full for speech, but the inexpressible relief he felt showed in his face and his blue eyes. "I'm glad you takes it like that, mother," he said simply, "I was afraid."

"Afraid! afraid of what? That I shouldn't want her!"

But at that moment the kettle boiled over with a great hiss, and brought them back to everyday affairs again.

"Well, any way," said Thomas, with a happy smile on his pleasant old face, "we can allow ourselves time for a bit of breakfast, or maybe when she does come we shall be past speaking a word to show her she's welcome," and while both of them laughed over his little joke, he made the long-delayed cup of tea, and, though both were too excited to eat, they sat down together to their breakfast.

CHAPTER II
JESSIE ARRIVES

Unwell though she had been, Mrs. Dawson would not let her husband do a single thing indoors to help her in preparation for the little newcomer.

"No. Men is only in the way," she said decidedly. "I shall get on twice as fast if you leave me the place to myself." So, knowing that she meant what she said, Thomas went out and set to work in the garden, for, of course, that must be made trim, too, for the little five-year-old grandchild. He forked over the earth in all the beds, tied up to a stick every daffodil that did not stand perfectly upright by itself, trimmed the sweetbriar hedge, and swept the paths.

"If I'd got the time," he called in to Patience, "I would give the gate a coat of paint."

"I wish you could," she called back, "and the front door, too, it'd be the better for it. To a stranger, I dare say it'll look shabby."

Evidently they expected the new-comer to be a very critical little person.

"I can whitewash the back porch," thought Thomas, "and I'll do it without saying anything to mother. It will be a bit of a surprise to her."

But while he was putting on the last brushful or two, a thought came to him which sent him hurrying into the house in quite a flurry.

"Mother!" he called up the stairs, "mother! we don't know when she's coming, Lizzie didn't say—and what's to prevent her coming to-day?"

Patience dropped her scrubbing-brush and sat down on the top stair, overcome with excitement and surprise. "To-day! this very day! Oh dear! oh dear! how careless of Lizzie not to tell us! The poor child might come at any time, and nobody be there to meet her, and we can't write and ask, for she didn't give us any address to write to. Lizzie did use to have some sense before she took up with that Harry Lang, but now—"

Patience lapsed into silence because she could not find words which would sufficiently express her feelings. She was tired and irritable too, and she never could endure uncertainty.

Thomas had been standing by all this while, thinking deeply. "Well," he said at last, "it's my belief she'd send her off as soon as she could after she'd wrote the letter, for if Lizzie had a hard thing to do, she was one as couldn't stop to think much about it, or she'd never do it at all. She's put London on the top of her letter, and the London train comes in at four-fifteen, and I'm thinking I'd better go and meet it, any way, and then, if the child don't come by it, I can tell Station-Master I'm expecting my little grandchild, but I don't know exactly when, and when she do come, will he keep her safe if I ain't there in time. I can't think of nothing better than that."

Patience rose briskly, with a look of relief on her face. There was something very wonderful in the thought that before another night she might be holding her own little grandchild in her arms. "What a head-piece you have got, father!" she cried admiringly. "Well, I mustn't stay here talking, or I shan't be ready. If I'd got the time I'd have whitened the ceiling and put a clean pretty paper on the walls of the little room."

"Little room!—are—are you giving her—Lizzie's room?" There was a note of shock or dismay in Thomas's voice.

"Yes," said Patience shortly. "The child must have a room, of course, and there isn't any other!" she answered shortly, because it hurt her to say what she had to, and she knew it would hurt Thomas even more to hear it. Lizzie's little bedroom had never been looked into by him since Lizzie had run away and left them, and Patience herself had only gone in now and then, when, for the sake of her own pride in her cottage, and to prevent her neighbour's comments, the window had to be cleaned and a fresh muslin blind put up.

She returned to the room now, and with a few deft touches, a turn and a twist or two, she moved the little bed and the bits of furniture out of their usual positions, and into some they had never occupied before. "Now it won't remind him so much," she said softly to herself, "it looks quite different," and she went out leaving door and window wide, for the sun and the soft breeze to play through.

With this new joy and the music she carried in her heart, her hands and feet flew through their work, so that by three o'clock the spotless stairs were scrubbed, and the neat kitchen made even neater, and Patience herself was ready to change her gown and put herself tidy.

Thomas was still busy in the garden. She did not know what about, but soon after she had gone up to her room she heard him calling her.

"What is it, father?" she called back. "I am up-stairs."

"I—I've got a little rose-bush that I've been bringing on in a pot, I—I thought," he concluded shyly, "I—thought the little maid would fancy it, perhaps, in her room."

A mist of tears dimmed Patience's eyes for a moment. "Bless his dear old heart," she said to herself softly, "how he thinks of everything." Aloud, she said heartily, "Why, of course she would, father. She'd be sure to love it, a real plant of her own! Will you put it up there, on the window-ledge? I've got my dress off, and I can't come for a minute," she added casually, in a tone very different from the eagerness with which she listened to hear if he did so.

"It would be a good time for him to break through, and go into the room again," she thought to herself. But Thomas did not fall in with her little scheme.

"I'll put it on the top stair, where you can see it," he called up, "and I'll go and tidy myself now, and make a start for the station. I shan't be so very much too soon."

"Only half-an-hour or so," said Patience to herself with a smile. Aloud she said, "I think you're wise, father, then you'll be able to take it easy on the way, and to explain to Station-Master all about it, in case she don't come, and I expect you'll find she won't be here for a day or two."

They kept on telling each other that, to try and prevent themselves from counting on it too much.

"No, I don't see how she can come to-day, but I'll step along to see the train come in; it'll satisfy our minds. We shouldn't feel happy to shut up the house and go to bed if we didn't know for certain."

So Thomas started off with a calm, businesslike air, outwardly, but inside him his heart was beating fast with expectation, and his step grew quicker and quicker as soon as he was out of sight of his own cottage windows.

He slackened his pace a little when he came within sight of the station, for it looked as quiet and sleepy as though no train was expected for ages yet; and the eager, shy old man felt that the men at the station would laugh at him for arriving more than half-an-hour before any train was due. For a moment he decided to turn away and walk in some other direction until some of the time had passed, but the seats on the platform looked very restful, and the platform, bathed in the soft afternoon sunshine, looked wonderfully peaceful and inviting. There was not a sign of life, or a sound or a movement, except that of the little breeze ruffling the young leaves on the chestnuts in the road outside.

"I'll explain to Mr. Simmons that I come early so as to be able to tell him about the little maid, while he'd got a few spare minutes before the train came in," he decided, and, with a sigh of relief, made his way into the station. He was tired after his exciting, busy day, and glad to sit down alone, to think over all that the day had brought them, and was likely to bring them.

Mr. Simmons, the station-master, must have been tired too, though his day had been neither busy nor exciting, for when at last he did appear, he was stretching and yawning as though the nap he had been having in his office had not been quite long enough for him.

When he saw Thomas his eye brightened, and he joined him at once, for he dearly loved a gossip, and he had in his mind a long story that he was impatient to pour out to somebody. The story was so long and so interesting that the whistle of the fast-approaching train was heard long before it was ended, and of his own story Thomas had not been able to tell a word.

"Is that the London train?" he asked eagerly, starting to his feet.

"It is, sir. Are you going by it?"

"No—o, oh no," said Thomas. His face flushed and his hands shook as a carriage door opened here and there and a passenger got out.

"Are 'ee expecting somebody?" asked the station-master, with just a touch of impatience in his voice. He did not approve of this reserve in Thomas, just after he had confided all that story to him too.

"Well, I hardly know," said Thomas slowly. "I am, and I ain't." A dull sick feeling of bitter disappointment filling his heart as he saw that beyond the two men who had sprung out at once, no one else was appearing. "I was going to tell 'ee about it, only the train corned in. I'm—I'm expecting my little granddaughter. She may come any day, by any train, so far as we know, for they—her mother, at least, forgot to say which."

The station-master, seeing that his presence was not required by the new arrivals, stood ready to listen to Thomas's story. "Didn't tell you when to expect her!" he exclaimed in surprise.

"No—o," said Thomas reluctantly. He shrank from talking about it, for fear Mr. Simmons would ask questions he did not want, or was unable, to answer. "She overlooked it, I reckon; and there hasn't been time to write and get an answer, so I thought I'd just step up and see this train in."

"Well, we may as well go the length of her and make sure," said Mr. Simmons, "if the child is very young, she may be afraid to move, or p'raps she doesn't know that this is where she ought to get out."

Fresh hope rose in Thomas's heart as they made their way along the whole length of the train. The guard and the porter paused in their gossip to turn and look at them, the engine-driver hanging lazily over the side of his box watched them idly. Thomas, who was filled now with fear that the engine would start off at a wild pace before they had time to search the carriages, was somewhat relieved by the lazy look of them all.

"Do you know if there was any little girl on board booked to Springbrook?" Mr. Simmons asked the guard as they drew near him.

"Why, yes, I b'lieve there was," answered the man casually. "Got in at St. Pancras. Hasn't she got out?"

"No."

Thomas hurried on more quickly. If she was booked for Springbrook, and wasn't in the train, no one knew what might have happened to her. She might have fallen out, or been stolen, or she might have got out at the wrong station, and a terrible fear weighed on him as he hurried on.

"Hi! Mr. Dawson, come here! Is this of her, do you think?"

Thomas ran along the platform to the carriage where the station-master stood, and both looked in. The compartment was empty, save for a little figure, huddled up fast asleep in one corner. Thomas looked at her, and his eyes grew misty. "Ye—es, that's of her," he answered. He hesitated, not because he doubted, for, though the little face was flushed and tear-stained, and the dark hair all rumpled about it, it might have been his own little Lizzie again.

The men looked from the child to each other helplessly. "What had we best do?" said the station-master, in a tone lowered so that it might not waken the little sleeper. "If she opens her eyes and sees us all here she'll be frightened."

"And if I touch her it'll wake her up with a start," said her grandfather anxiously. But before they had settled the knotty point, the engine-driver, growing tired of waiting, let off a shrill whistle from his engine and with the sound the little sleeper stirred, opened her eyes, and sat up suddenly. The porter hastily disappeared from the doorway, the station-master left the carriage too, but the guard remained, and nodded and smiled at her reassuringly.

"You remember me, don't you, little one! I've brought you all the way home, and here we are, and here is grandfather come to see you."

Jessie sat up and looked from one to the other with troubled eyes. "I want mother," she said at last, with piteously trembling lips.

"Oh, now, you ain't going to cry again, are you?" cried the guard, pretending to be shocked. "Good little girls don't cry. 'Tis time to get out, too, the train is going on, and you'll be carried away, if you don't mind what you're about, and then how will mother ever be able to find you? Come along, get up like a good little maid."

Poor Jessie, really frightened at the thought of such a fearful possibility, turned piteously to her grandfather, who had been all this time standing by awkwardly, wondering what he could do or say. But at that look he forgot himself and his doubts, and the guard and everything but the pitiful frightened look on the little face.

"Come along with grandfather," he said coaxingly, dropping on his knee beside her. "Come along with me, dear, and I'll take care of you till mother comes. Granny is home waiting for 'ee with a bootiful tea, and there's flowers, and a kitten, and a fine little rose-bush in a pot that grandfather picked out on purpose for 'ee. Wouldn't you like to come and see it all?"

"Will Jessie have roses?" she asked eagerly, her eyes growing bright and expectant.

"Yes, I shouldn't be surprised if there's one nearly out already. Let's go home quick, and see, shall we? It had got a bud on it when I left, maybe it'll be out by this time, if not you can be sure it will be to-morrow."

The engine gave another shrill whistle, the train jerked and quivered. Thomas hastily gathered up Jessie in his arms, shawl and all. "Where's your box, and all the rest of it?"

"Haven't got any."

"Haven't got any! Your clothes, I mean, frocks and hats and boots and suchlike."

"I've got on my boots," putting out her feet, and showing a very shabby broken pair, "and there's a parcel there, my old frock is in it, and my pinny, that's all."

Thomas picked up the parcel, and hurried out of the already slowly-moving train.

"Tickets, please," said the man at the gate.

"Have 'ee got your ticket?" Thomas inquired anxiously.

"Yes," she nodded; "but you must put me down, please; it is in my purse, and my purse is in my pocket, and I can't get at it while you are holding me."

Her grandfather did as he was told, and Jessie, freeing herself from the great shawl which enveloped her, shook out her frock, and diving her hand into her pocket, drew out an old shabby purse. The clasp was broken, and it was tied round with a piece of string, but her little fingers quickly undid this, and from the inside pocket drew out her railway ticket and a ha'penny. In giving the porter the ticket she had some trouble not to give him the ha'penny too.

"I can't give you my money," she explained gravely, "for it is all I've got, but I had to put it in there with the ticket, because there's a hole in my purse that side, do you see?" and she showed it to the man, pushing her finger through the hole that he might see it better. "It was mother's purse, but she lost a sixpence one day, and then she gave it to me. It does all right for me, 'cause I only have pennies," she explained gravely as she put her purse back into her pocket again.

The porter agreed. "'Tis a nice purse for a little girl," he said quite seriously; "there's heaps of wear in it yet, by the look of it."

Thomas Dawson stood by, his face all alight with smiles and interest. "What a clever little maid 'tis," he thought, "and what a happy little soul to be so ready to talk like that right away."

"Now, my dear, are 'ee ready? We must hurry on, or granny'll think you ain't come, and she will be wondering what's become of me. Shall I carry you again?"

"No, thank you, I'd like to walk, but I'd like you to hold my hand. Mother always does; she's afraid I'll get lost with so many people about."

"Well, you won't be troubled with too many people hereabouts," said her grandfather, laughing, but he was only too glad to clasp the little hand thrust into his, and they walked on very happily together talking quite as though they were old friends.

"We are nearly home now, 'tisn't so very much further. Are 'ee tired, dear?"

"No—o, not so very," she answered, but in rather a weary voice. "Are you too tired to carry me?"

Her grandfather laughed, but before he could reply, or pick her up, she drew back a little. "Is my face clean?" she asked anxiously. "I must have a clean face when I see granny. Mother told me granny doesn't like little girls with dirty faces. Do you, granp?"

"I like some little girls, no matter what their faces is like," he said warmly, but recollecting himself, he added quickly, "Of course I like 'em best with nice clean faces and hands and tidy hair. Every one does."

"Mother said you didn't mind so much," she added brightly.

"Did she! did she now! Just fancy her thinking that!" The old man's face quite lighted up at the thought of Lizzie's remembering. "Yes, I used to dip the corner of my handkerchief in the brook sometimes and wash her little face for her, so as she might go home to her mother looking clean. Look, here is a little brook, shall I wash yours over a bit, like I used to mother's?"

"Oh, please, please," cried Jessie delightedly.

So by the wayside they stopped and made quite a little toilette, her face and hands were washed, and her hair put back neatly under her shabby hat, and then they went on again.

Patience Dawson, looking anxiously out of the window, saw them at last arrive at the gate, and her heart almost stood still with excitement and nervousness. "Why, it might be five and twenty years ago, and Thomas be bringing in Lizzie herself!" she gasped. Her face flushed, tears suddenly brimmed over and down her cheeks. She longed to run down the garden and take the little child in her arms and hold her to her heart, but a sudden shyness came over her and held her fast. She could only stand there and watch them and wait.

She saw her husband looking eagerly from window to door, expecting to see her; she saw the little child face turned excitedly from side to side, exclaiming at the sight of the flowers, and sniffing in the scent.

"Oh, granp, smell the 'warriors'!" she heard her cry in a perfectly friendly voice. "You sniff hard and you'll smell them. Oh, my!"

"She's friends with him already, same as Lizzie was. I wish I knew how to—" But her wish she only sighed, she did not put it into words.

"Never mind the flowers now, little maid; here's granny inside waiting for us." Then he put her down on her feet, and led her over the threshold.

Patience, dabbing the tears from her eyes with her handkerchief, stepped forward to meet them. "I'd begun to wonder what had become of 'ee, father," she said. "I s'pose the train was late. Well, dear," stooping to kiss her little grandchild, "how are you? Have you got a kiss for granny?"

"Yes," Jessie nodded gravely, "and my face is very clean," she added, as she put it up to be kissed. But she turned and slipped her hand into her grandfather's again as soon as the kiss was given, for she felt a little awed and shy with this granny, who seemed so much more grown-up and stern than did the grandfather.

Her shyness did not last very long, though; by the time granny had taken her up to her room and shown her the rose-bush, and taken off her hat and brushed out her hair, and brought her down to tea and lifted her into her seat at the table, much of her shyness had worn off, and the sight of the mug with pictures on it, and the little plate "with words on it," loosened her tongue again, and set it chattering quite freely.

The meal lasted a long time that night, for Jessie was full of talk, and neither her "granp," as she already familiarly called him, nor her granny could bear to interrupt her, especially after she had slidden down from her high seat at the table, and clambered on to her grandfather's knee; for to them her presence seemed like some wonderful dream, from which they were afraid of waking.

At last, though, the little tongue grew quiet, the dark curly head fell back on granp's shoulder, and then the bright eyes closed.

"I reckon I'd best carry her right up to bed," said Thomas softly. "If I hand her over to you she'll waken, as sure as anything."

Patience only nodded, she could not speak, her heart was so full, and rising she followed him up the stairs, carrying the lamp. At the door of Lizzie's old room she expected him to stop and hand the sleeping child over to her, but, apparently without remembering what room it was, he walked straight in, and very tenderly laid his burthen on the bed. Then, with a glance at the rose-bush on the sill, he crept softly out and down the stairs again.

Patience stood by her little sleeping grandchild with tears of joy in her eyes. "She's broke his will," she said gladly, "for her sake he's forgotten. P'raps now he'll get over the trouble, and forget, and be happier again."

CHAPTER III
SHOPPING AND TEAING

The next morning some of Jessie's shyness had returned, but it vanished again at the sight of the mug with the pictures and the plate with the "words" on it. At the liberal dishful of bacon and eggs she stared wide-eyed.

"You can eat a slice of bacon and an egg, can't you, dearie?" asked her granny.

"Yes, please!" with a sigh of pleasure. "May I?"

"Why, of course," said granny heartily. "Why not? Do you like eggs?"

Jessie nodded. "I had one once, a whole one, but that was for my dinner. We don't ever have eggs for breakfast at home," she added impressively.

"Don't you?" answered her grandfather gravely, "then what do you have? Something you like better, I s'pose?"

He did not ask from curiosity, that was the last thing he would have been guilty of; he only wanted to show an interest and to hear her talk.

"We don't have nuffin', 'cepts when father has got work, then father has a bloater. Me and mother have one too, sometimes, then. But when father is out of work we only has bread."

Patience turned pale, and Thomas groaned. Jessie looked up with quick sympathy. "Have you hurted your toof, granp?" she asked gravely, little dreaming that it was she herself who had given him pain.

"No, my dear, granp's all right. Try and make a good breakfast now. You've got to get as plump and round as the kitten over there."

Patience had laid down her knife and fork, and sat staring before her with miserably troubled eyes. "It seems wrong to be eating, when— when there's others—one's own, too—going hungry!"

"Nonsense now," said Thomas gruffly; "don't 'ee talk like that, mother, it's foolish. We've got to think of ourselves and those about us, and it's our duty to eat and drink and be sensible, whether we likes it or not." He spoke gruffly, because he felt that if he spoke in any other way, he or Patience would break down.

Jessie came to their help, though. "My rose is nearly out, granp," she announced proudly, as soon as she was able to lift her thoughts from the wonderful experience of having an egg *and* bacon for breakfast. "I saw it all showing pink. I expect by the time we've finished our breakfases it will be right wide out. You come up and see too, will you?"

And sure enough when breakfast was really done, she took his hand in hers and led him up and into the room he had shunned so long.

"I don't think it will be full out until to-morrow," he decided; but Jessie couldn't help thinking he had made a mistake, and many times that day she climbed the stairs to see, and was quite troubled when at last she had to go to bed, for fear the bud would open while her eyes were shut.

"I think it is a very slow rose," she said, shaking her head sagely as her granny was undressing her. "I am sure it *ought* to have been out by this time."

And then, after all her watching, the bud burst into full bloom before Jessie was awake the next morning. When she opened her eyes and saw it she felt quite vexed. "I wish I had put you back in a dark corner," she said to it, "then you wouldn't have opened till I was awake."

"The little maid is a born gardener," chuckled her grandfather, when he was told of it; "'tis the folk that talks to their flowers that gets the best out of them."

"If talking'll do it, her rose-bush will be covered thick, then," laughed her grandmother.

"I wish I could send some of my roses to mother," sighed Jessie; "mother loves roses," and the tears came into her eyes. "Granny, do you think my roses will all be gone before mother comes for me?"

"Your—mother! Is she coming?" Patience was so taken aback that she spoke in almost a dismayed tone, and Jessie, with her loving little heart and quick ears, noticed it and was hurt. It sounded to her as though her granny did not want her mother; and her chin quivered and her eyes filled, for she wanted her mother very much, and every one else should want her too, she thought.

Her grandfather saw the poor little quivering lips and tear-filled eyes, and understood. "The rose may be past," he said cheerfully, "for the time, any way, but we'll have flowers of some kind ready for mother whenever she comes. 'Tis you and I, little maid, will see to that, won't we? We must make it our business to have something blooming all the year round, then we'll be sure to be right."

Jessie looked up at him gratefully, and the tears changed to smiles. Something told her that granp would be glad to see mother whenever she came. The thought of growing flowers for her was a lovely one, too; it seemed to bring her mother nearer; and, though granny and granp were so kind, oh, she did want her so very, very much. She wanted her to see the garden and the house, and the kitten, and to have bacon and eggs for breakfast, and milk in her tea, and nice butter on her bread.

Then, in the midst of these thoughts, something that granny was saying caught her attention, and, for the moment, drove all other thoughts out of her head.

"I've been thinking I'd better go into Norton this afternoon, and do some shopping," she remarked to granp, "for the child must have some clothes, and as soon as possible, too; and I reckon I'd better take her with me, though she really isn't fit, her boots and her hat are so shabby; but it'll be better to have her there to be fitted, especially the first time."

"Oh, she doesn't look so bad," answered granp cheerfully. "If she keeps smiling at folks they won't notice her hat nor her boots neither."

Granny was not so sure of that. Her pride was a little hurt at the thought of taking such a shabbily-clad little granddaughter into the shops where she was well known. However, hats and boots required to be tried on, so there was nothing for it but to make the best of things, and Jessie was to be taken to Norton.

What a day of wonders that was to Jessie! It seemed almost as though there were too many good things crowded into one twenty-four hours.

As soon as it was decided that they were to go, her grandfather went off and borrowed Mrs. Maddock's donkey and the little cart, to drive them in, for Norton was more than a mile and a half away, and that was too far, they thought, for Jessie's little feet to walk. So the cart was brought, and granny and grandfather sat on the little wooden seat, while Jessie sat on a rug in the bottom of the cart, at their feet. She liked it better there, she thought, for there was no fear of her falling out, and she could look all about her and feel quite safe and comfortable all the time. Granp gave her the whip to hold, but she had no work to do, for Moses, the donkey, behaved so well, he never once needed it all the way to Norton.

Jessie was very glad, for she could not bear to think of anything being punished on such a lovely afternoon. The birds were singing, the hedges were covered with little green leaves, just bursting forth. Here and there a blackthorn bush was in full flower, and filled Jessie with delight. She sat very quiet, looking about her with a serious happy face, drinking it all in, and evidently thinking deeply. Her grandfather watched her with the keenest interest.

"I reckon it looks funny to you, don't it, little maid, after all the streets and houses and bustle you've been accustomed to?" he asked at last.

Jessie nodded. "There's such lots of room, and no peoples," she said soberly, "and at home there was such lots of peoples and no room. Where are they all gone, granp?"

"Gone to London, I reckon," answered granp, with a laugh.
"You'll find it quiet, and you'll miss the shops, little maid."

"Shops!" said granny indignantly; "we shall be in Norton in a little while now, and there's shops enough there to satisfy any one, I should hope."

But when they reached the little town, and Jessie was lifted down from the cart, and put to stand in the street while granny dismounted, she looked about her, wondering greatly where the shops could be. There did not seem to be many people here either. Two sauntered up to look at the donkey-cart, and to pass the time of day with Mr. Dawson, but that was all. There were no omnibuses, no motors, no incessant tramp, tramp, tramp, of horses' hoofs, making the never-ceasing dull roar to which she had been accustomed all her life, and Jessie missed it. Suddenly she felt very lonely and forlorn. The world was so big and empty and silent, and her mother so very, very far away. There seemed to be nobody left to see, or care, or hear, no matter what happened.

But just at the moment when her tears were nearly brimming over, she heard her grandfather say proudly, "Yes, this is Jessie, my little grandchild, Lizzie's little girl," and turning her head she saw him holding out his hand to her, and all was well once more. With granp's big hand holding hers so closely she could not feel that no one heard or cared, and the day looked all bright and sunny again.

She felt sorry when her grandfather mounted into the little cart to drive home, and she almost wished she was going with him; but granny, taking her by the hand, led her quickly down the street and into a draper's shop.

Jessie felt rather shy when her grandmother led her in, for though she had spent a lot of time looking at shop windows with her mother, she had very seldom been inside one, and when she had gone in the places had been so full of people always that no one had paid any heed to her, which was what she liked. But here she and her grandmother seemed to be almost the only customers that afternoon, and all the assistants looked at them as they entered. They all smiled, too, and most of them said, "Good-afternoon, Mrs. Dawson," in a very friendly way, which only made Jessie feel even more uncomfortable, for she realized suddenly that her boots were cracked, and her hat very shabby, and that she had no gloves at all; and she wished very much that they could get right away up to the far end of the shop, where it seemed quite empty and quiet.

Mrs. Dawson apparently wished the same, for though she gave a smile and a greeting to all, she walked sturdily through the shop, ignoring the chairs pulled out for her by the polite shop-walker, and made her way to the very end, where a pleasant-faced attendant stood alone, rolling up ribbons in a leisurely way.

"Well, Mrs. Dawson," she said brightly, "you *are* a stranger. I hope you are well? And who is this little person? Not your granddaughter, surely?"

"Yes, it is. This is Lizzie's little girl," said Mrs. Dawson, a faint flush rising to her cheeks. "She is come to stay with us for a good long spell."

"Well, the country air will do her good. She looks rather thin."

"She does," agreed Mrs. Dawson, looking at Jessie with kindly anxious eyes, "but she looks healthy, I think, don't you?" Already it gave her a pang to hear any one say that her Jessie did not look well.

"Oh yes!" agreed the girl reassuringly. "What can I get for you to-day, Mrs. Dawson?"

"Well," said Mrs. Dawson thoughtfully, "it seems to me I want a good many things. What I want mostly is some clothes for Jessie. Living in the country, she ought to have something that'll wear well, strong boots, and a plain sun-hat, and some print for washing-frocks."

Jessie's eyes opened wider and wider. Were all those things really to be bought for her? It seemed impossible; but the girl, who did not seem at all overcome, went off as though it were quite an ordinary matter, and presently she returned with an armful of pretty soft straw hats with wide drooping brims, and tried them one by one over Jessie's curls.

"I declare, any of them would suit her; but I think she'd look sweet in that one," she said at last, and granny agreed.

"What would you trim it with?" she asked; "a bit of plain ribbon, I should think." But the girl shook her head.

"Oh no, if I was you I'd have a little wreath of flowers round it; it would make ever so pretty a hat, and would last her for Sundays right on till the late autumn. I'll show you some;" and dragging out a big drawer, she displayed a perfect garden of dainty blossoms, daisies, roses, forget-me-nots, moss, ferns, and flowers of every kind that ever grew, and many kinds that never did or could grow.

Jessie's eyes, though, were caught by a wreath of feathery moss with little blue forget-me-nots peeping out of it here and there, and when she was asked which she liked best, she decidedly picked out that one. To her great delight her granny's taste agreed with her, and the wreath and the hat and a piece of white ribbon were put aside together.

"Now," laughed Mrs. Dawson, "I've got to get her another for every day. That's a pretty fine thing! I reckon you think there's no bottom to my purse!"

"Now, Mrs. Dawson, you won't regret spending that money, I am sure," said the attendant coaxingly; "and this one shan't cost more than eighteenpence, trimming and all," and she produced a big shady-brimmed, flexible straw, for which was shown as trimming a pretty soft flowered ribbon, to be loosely twisted around the crown. Then came a length of blue serge for a warm dress, and two pieces of print, one with blue flowers all over it, and the other with pink ones. Jessie thought them both perfectly lovely, and while they were being chosen she slid off her chair and went and leaned against her grandmother. She did not feel at all afraid of her now; she felt that she wanted to kiss her for all her kindness, and to tell her how grateful she was. She did not do that, she was still too shy, but Mrs. Dawson seemed to understand, for she put her arm very fondly about her, and drew her very close.

"Now, if only you could sew," she said, "you'd be able to help me finely with all this, but I s'pose I shall get it done somehow. I must let other things go for the time."

Jessie longed eagerly to be able to help, but she couldn't sew at all, she had never even tried. She thought, though, that she might be able to do some of the other things granny mentioned, and she made up her mind to do her best. She wouldn't say anything to any one, but she would try, and she grew quite excited at the thought.

"I wish mother knew," she sighed presently, when the assistant had gone off to get the boots for her to try on. "Mother tried to get me a new hat, but she hadn't got any money. She would be so glad to know what lots of nice new things I am having." Then, as she saw the girl approaching from a distant part of the shop, she put up her arm to draw her grandmother's head down to her own level. "Mother cried when she sent me away," she whispered solemnly, "because she couldn't get me any new clothes."

When the assistant reached them again, with her arms full of boots, she found Mrs. Dawson rubbing her eyes and nose violently with her large white cotton handkerchief.

"You haven't got a cold, I hope," the girl asked sympathetically, but Mrs. Dawson reassured her.

After the boots had been fitted, a pair of felt slippers was brought and added to the collection; then sundry yards of calico and flannel, and brown holland, some stockings, and what Jessie thought the most wonderful of all, a pair of cotton gloves and some little handkerchiefs with coloured borders.

By the time all this was done both Mrs. Dawson and Jessie felt that they had had enough shopping for one day. "And if I have forgotten anything, well, Norton isn't so far off but what we can come again," laughed Mrs. Dawson, refusing to listen to anything the pleasant-faced girl tried to tempt her with.

"Shawls, umbrellas, caps, sheets—"

"No, none of them, thank you," said granny decidedly.

The proprietor of the shop came up. "Now, I am sure, Mrs. Dawson, you must want something for the master?" he urged smilingly.

"No, I don't," said granny. "Thomas has got to make the best of what he has got. All I want now is a cup of tea, and I must go and get it, and see about making our way home."

"Well," said Mr. Binns, "I am sure this little person can find a use for one of these," and he picked up a little silk scarf with a flower worked in each corner, and laid it across Jessie's shoulders.

Jessie looked up, speechless with delight. "Well, I never!"
Mrs. Dawson exclaimed; "now, that is kind of you, Mr.
Binns. I'm sure Jessie'll be proud enough of that, won't you,
Jessie?"

"Oh yes, thank you," said Jessie earnestly. "I'll—I'll only wear it for best."

At which Mr. Binns and Mrs. Dawson and the pleasant-faced girl all laughed, Jessie didn't know why, and then granny said "good-bye," and she and Jessie made their way out into the street. The afternoon sun was fading by this time, and the shadows had grown long.

"I do want my tea badly, don't you?" said granny again.

"Yes," sighed Jessie, for she was really very tired, "but it doesn't matter," she hastened to add. It was what she used to say to her mother to comfort her when there was little or no food in the house.

"But it does matter," said granny decidedly; "we have a longish walk before us, and we shan't get anything for another couple of hours or so, if we don't have it now. So we'll go and have a nice tea at once. Come along," and she led the way further down the street until they came to a baker's shop, from which there floated out a delicious smell of hot cakes and pastry.

Behind the shop there was an old-fashioned, low-ceilinged room with small tables and chairs dotted about it. At one of these Mrs. Dawson and Jessie seated themselves, and soon a kindly-faced woman brought in a tray with a brown teapot of tea, a jug of milk, and a goodly supply of cakes and bread and butter.

Jessie had never been in such a place before, and she felt there could be nothing grander or more interesting in the whole world. In the shop outside people were coming and going, and one or two came in and seated themselves at other little tables, and Jessie sat and watched it all with the greatest interest, while she ate and drank as much as ever she wanted of the nice bread and butter and fascinating cakes.

"I wish mother could see me now," she sighed at last. "And oh, wouldn't it be nice if she was here, too. She'd love a beautiful tea like this."

Patience Dawson did not know what reply to make, her feelings brought a sob to her throat, and the old ache back to her heart.

"Oh, I expect she is having quite as good a tea as we are," she said at last, for want of something else to say. But Jessie shook her head sagely.

"I don't 'spect she is; we didn't have tea—only sometimes, and we never had cake, never!"

"Well, p'raps mother and you and me will all come here together one day," she said, trying to speak cheerfully, though she little expected such a thing to happen.

"And granp too?" said Jessie eagerly.

"Oh yes, granp too, of course." But her grandmother noticed that she never once expressed a wish that her father should join them.

When at last the meal was over, and Mrs. Dawson had paid the bill and talked a little with the woman who had served them, they made their way slowly into the street.

"I think," said Mrs. Dawson musingly, standing still and turning things over in her mind, "I think we had better go home by train; 'tis a good step, a mile and a half, for you to walk, and for me, too, with all these parcels; it isn't nearly so far to walk home from the station." So two days following Jessie arrived at Springbrook station, and when she got out of the train the station-master and the porter both recognized her and smiled at her.

"Why, you've become quite a traveller, missie," said Mr. Simmons jokingly; "supposing we had let you sleep on! where would you have been by this time, I wonder?"

"I don't know," answered Jessie, looking quite alarmed.

"I hope you've got your purse safe, missie," said the porter, as he passed her.

"Yes, thank you," answered Jessie gravely, putting her hand down and feeling it in her pocket.

"Good-night!" they all said to each other as they parted, which Jessie thought was very polite and friendly of them. Then she and her granny stepped out into the road, and walked quickly through the fast-deepening twilight to the little cottage where the light was already glowing a welcome to them from the kitchen window, and grandfather was waiting supper for them.

CHAPTER IV
A GARDEN SUNDAY-SCHOOL

Springbrook village lay near Springbrook station. It was a very small village, but those who lived in it thought it a very pretty one. It consisted of the church, the vicarage, the doctor's house, three or four small private houses and a number of picturesque cottages.

The church stood at one end of the village in the middle of a beautiful churchyard and burying-ground, surrounded by fine trees— flowering chestnuts and sweet-scented limes, while every here and there blossomed beautiful red May-trees, lilacs, laburnums, syringas and roses. From this, the one street—lined on either side by little cottages, with here and there a small shop—led to the green, around which stood in irregular fashion pretty houses and large cottages with gardens before their doors. The doctor lived in one of these houses, and the curate, Mr. Harburton, in another, and Miss Barley and Miss Grace Barley in a third, and all the houses looked out on the green and the road and across at each other, but all those who dwelt in them were so neighbourly and friendly, this did not matter at all.

Jessie thought the houses by the green were perfectly lovely, they had creepers and roses growing over them, and window-boxes full of flowers. She thought the green was lovely too, and almost wished that she lived by it that she might be able to see the donkeys and the ducks which were usually standing about cropping the grass, or poking about in the little stream which ran along one side of the green. She thought the ivy-covered church, with the trees and the hawthorns all about it, one of the most beautiful sights in the world, and nothing she loved better than to walk with granp along the sweet-scented roads along by the green and through the village street to church.

Mrs. Dawson did not go in the morning, as a rule. "Grandfather must have a nice hot dinner once a week," she declared, so she stayed at home to cook it; but they all went together to the evening service, and Jessie dearly loved the walk to church in the quiet summer's evening, with granp and granny on either side of her, and home again through the gathering twilight, sweet with the scent from the gardens and hedges.

Sometimes, when they got home, granny would give them their supper in the garden, if the weather was very warm, and Jessie loved this. While granny was helping her on with her big print overall, grandfather would carry out two big arm-chairs, and a little one for Jessie, and there they would sit, with their plates on their laps and their mugs beside them, and eat and talk until darkness or the falling dew drove them in.

Sometimes they repeated hymns, verse and verse, first grandfather, then granny, and by and by, as she came to know them, Jessie herself would take her turn too. Sometimes they would repeat a psalm or two in the same way, or a chapter, and before very long they had taught Jessie some of these also, so that, to her great delight, she could join in with them.

Then came bedtime, when she knelt in her little white nightgown beside her bed and repeated—

> "Gentle Jesus, meek and mild,
> Look upon a little child,
> Pity my simplicity,
> Suffer me to come to Thee
> Fain I would to Thee be brought;
> Dearest God, forbid it not;
> But in the kingdom of Thy grace
> Grant a little child her place.

"Pray God bless dear father and mother, grandfather and grandmother, and all kind friends and relations, and help me to be a good girl, for Christ's sake. Amen."

Then, with one look at her rose to see if there were any more buds on it, and a glance into the garden to see if grandfather was still there, she lay down in her little white bed, and with a kiss from granny and a last good-night she would be asleep almost before granny had reached the foot of the stairs.

Then when morning came Jessie was just as glad to open her eyes and spring out of bed as she had been to spring into it, for life was full of all sorts of delights, indeed she would have liked nothing better than for it to go on and on always in the same happy way. With Mrs. Dawson, though, things were different. Granny began to grow very troubled about Jessie's education.

"It is time she was learning," she said anxiously, many a time. "I know she ought to go to Sunday-school regularly, but I don't know how it is to be managed. She can't walk there and back three times a day, I am sure. If she walked there and back in the morning, and there and back in the afternoon, she wouldn't be fit to go with us in the evening too. She would be tired out. We couldn't go to church in the evening either, for one of us would have to stay with her."

Grandfather sat for a few moments meditating deeply over this problem, then, "*I* can teach her myself for a bit on Sundays," he exclaimed triumphantly, his dear old face lighting up at the thought of it. "I know enough about the Bible and Prayer-book for that. It would do me good too."

"But there's her other schooling. What can we do about that?"

"I s'pose she'll have to do as the other children do," said grandfather gravely, "and walk there and back twice every day. Some of the bigger ones would let her walk with them, then she would be safe enough. We will begin our Sunday-school next Sunday"—his blue eyes lighting up with pleasure at the thought of it. The day-school was quite a secondary matter to him, with the idea of that other filling his mind. "We can sit in the garden while the fine weather lasts. It would be lovely there, and good for the little maid too."

So, when Sunday came, grandfather's big chair and Jessie's little one were carried out into the garden, and placed side by side, near the porch, and a little table was carried out, too, for grandfather's Bible and Prayer and hymn-books, and then, looking very pleased but serious, the pair seated themselves. The dear old man was a little bit shy and embarrassed, and very nervous when it actually came to the point, and for a moment he looked more like a new shy pupil than the teacher. Jessie was much the more composed of the two.

"When are you going to begin, granp?" she demanded anxiously.

"Now. I think we will begin with learning you the Lord's prayer," he said huskily, feeling that something was expected of him, and he must not fail. "Now, 'Our Father—'"

"I know that already," said Jessie reproachfully; "but why is it called the 'Lord's Prayer,' granp? Did the Lord have to say it when He was little?"

"No. He told it for all little children to say, all the world over, and big children too, and men and women."

Jessie looked awed and puzzled. "How did everybody all over the world know about it, granp? They couldn't all hear Him say it," she asked.

"No, and they don't all know it yet, though it's nearly one thousand nine hundred years ago since the Lord spoke it. But they will in time," said the old man softly, as though speaking to himself. "He left word with His people that they were to teach each other, and they did. You see there wasn't such a great many heard Him, but those that did went about and taught others, and then those they taught taught others again, and—"

"And then some one taught you, and," her face growing suddenly bright, "I'll have to teach somebody. Who shall I teach, granp? Granny knows it, doesn't she?"

Her grandfather smiled. "She knew it before she was your age, child," he said gently.

"Then I'll teach mother."

"Your mother knew it too before she was so old as you are."

"Did she?" said Jessie, surprised. "She never said anything to me about it, then."

"Well, hadn't we best be getting on with the lesson?" asked grandfather; "time is passing, and we haven't hardly begun yet."

Jessie settled back in her chair, and leaning her head against her grandfather, listened quietly while the old man talked reverently to her of her Father in heaven.

"Is He mother's 'our Father,' too, granp?" she asked at last.

"Yes, child, mother's and father's."

"Then He'll take care of her, won't He, and see that she doesn't cry too much for me?"

"Yes. He soothes all the sorrows and wipes away all the tears of them that love and trust Him. Now shall we read a hymn? I like the hymns dearly, don't you, little maid?"

"Oh yes, I love them," said Jessie, sitting up and clasping her hands eagerly. "Let's sing it, granp, shall we?"

"Go on, then. You take the lead."

"What's the lead, granp?" she asked anxiously.

"You start the tune. You begin and I'll join in."

But Jessie grew suddenly shy. "No, I—I can't," she said nervously, sliding her soft little hand into her grandfather's rough one as it lay on his knee. "You begin, granp, please—no, let's begin together, and we'll sing 'Safe in the arms of Jesus,' shall we? I know all of that."

So together rose the old voice and the young one, the first quavering and thin, the other tremulous and childlike, and floated out on the still warm summer air. Mrs. Dawson, reluctant to disturb them, waited in the kitchen with the tea-tray until they had ended, and the tears stood in her eyes as she listened.

"Bless them!" she murmured tenderly, "bless them both."

When the last notes had died away, and grandfather had closed the books and laid them one on top of the other, and their first Sunday-school might fairly be said to be closed, Jessie, looking up, saw her grandmother standing in the doorway, holding a snowy tablecloth in her hand.

"Tea-time!" cried Jessie delightedly, springing to her feet. "I'll carry away the books, granp, and help granny to bring out the tea-things. Now don't you move, you sit there and rest, we will do it all by ourselves."

So the old man, well pleased, sat on and watched his little granddaughter. There was nothing she loved better than to be busy, helping some one.

Such a tea it was, too, that she helped to bring out. First came granny with the tray, with the old-fashioned blue and white tea-set, Jessie's mug and a jug of milk, then followed Jessie with a plate of bread and butter. When all this was arranged, back they went again, soon to reappear, Mrs. Dawson with a delicious-looking apple-pie and a bowl of sugar, while to Jessie was entrusted, what she considered the most precious burthen of all—a dish of cream. And there, amidst the scents of the mignonette and stocks, the roses and jessamine, the Sunday twitter of the birds and hum of the bees, they sat and slowly enjoyed their Sunday meal, lingering over it in the full enjoyment of the peace and calm of the hour and the scene. And oh, how good the tea tasted, and the apple-pie and cream, and the bread and butter, all with the open-air flavour about them, which is better than any other.

Then, having eaten and drunk all they wanted, they sat back in their chairs and talked and listened to the birds and the bees, and gazed about them at the flowers close by and the hills in the distance, looking so far away and still and mysterious in the fading afternoon light. And as they sat there, little dreaming of what was about to happen, a graceful woman's figure came slowly along the sunny road to their gate and there paused.

"Why, it's Miss Grace Barley, I do declare!" cried Mrs. Dawson, rising hurriedly to her feet. "Go and open the gate for her, father, do. Why, whatever is she doing here, at this time of day? Sunday, too, and all. It is very kind of her, I am sure."

Patience began hurriedly gathering together the tea-things and carrying them into the house, Jessie helping her.

"Wouldn't Miss—the lady like some tart, granny?" she asked, as she saw her grandmother beginning to pick it up. To her it seemed that every one must hunger for anything so delicious. Somehow, too, it did not seem very kind to carry it all away from under their visitor's very eyes.

"Well, now, I declare, I never thought of that," said granny pausing and replacing the pie on the table, "at any rate, I can but ask her. I'll put the kettle on, in case she hasn't had any tea."

Meanwhile Thomas had let their visitor in and welcomed her warmly, and they came slowly up the path together, looking at the flowers as they passed. Jessie stood by her little chair, watching the lady. She knew she was the Miss Grace Barley who lived in one of the pretty houses by the green, and she thought she looked as pretty as the house and just right to live in it.

When they came close Miss Grace smiled at her, then stooped and kissed her. "You are Jessie, I know," she said kindly. "I have seen you in church with your granny and grandfather."

"Yes, miss," said Jessie shyly, not quite knowing what to say, but feeling that something was expected of her, "and I have seen you there."

Mrs. Dawson came out of the house, and Miss Grace shook hands with her. "You must wonder to see me here at this time of day, Mrs. Dawson," she said brightly. "The organist at Hanford is ill, and I have been out there to play the organ at the morning and afternoon services; I was on my way home when I caught sight of you all in your pretty garden, and I couldn't resist coming in to join you."

"I'm sure we're very glad you did, miss," said Patience warmly. "And you haven't had any tea yet, Miss Grace, I'll be bound now."

Miss Barley smiled and shook her head. "No, I have not, I am really on my way to it, but I would rather sit here for a few moments first, though, and talk to you."

"You can do both, miss, if you will," said Patience hospitably. "I was about to clear the tea-things away, thinking they looked untidy, when Jessie stopped me. She was sure you would like a piece of apple-pie and cream, and I was sure you'd like a cup of tea with it; so the kettle is on and I'll have a cup ready in a minute if you'll excuse my leaving you. Thomas, give Miss Grace a chair," and Patience bustled away into the house delighted.

Mr. Dawson brought out another chair, and he and Jessie seated themselves one on each side of their visitor. Miss Barley withdrew her admiring gaze from the distant view.

"Don't you love Sunday, Jessie?" she asked, laying her hand gently on the little girl's shoulder. "A Sunday like this, when even the birds and the cattle, and even the flowers seem to be more glad and happy and peaceful than usual."

"Oh yes," said Jessie, losing all her shyness at once, "speshally now when granp and me have Sunday-school out here. We are going to have it every Sunday, ain't we, granp? We shall have it out here when it is fine, but when winter comes we shall go in by the fire."

Miss Grace looked at Mr. Dawson inquiringly. "What a lovely plan," she cried enthusiastically. "Whose idea was it, yours, Mr. Dawson?" and Thomas, blushing a little, told her all about it.

Just as they had finished, granny came out with the tea-tray, and spreading the table again with a tempting meal, drew it up before their visitor, and while Miss Grace ate and drank, they sat and talked to her, and presently Mrs. Dawson poured into her sympathetic ear all their difficulties about the school for Jessie. Miss Grace listened with the greatest attention, the matter seemed to interest her immensely, far more, in fact, than it did Jessie, indeed Jessie wished very much that they would talk of something else, for Miss Grace grew quite quiet and thoughtful, and ceased to notice the pretty things about her, or to talk of things that were interesting to Jessie, and Jessie was sorry. She became interested enough, though, presently, when Miss Grace, having finished her tea and risen to go, suddenly said—

"Well, Mrs. Dawson, I think you will have to let me solve the difficulty of Jessie's education for you, and there is nothing I should like better. You see, our home is quite twenty minutes' walk nearer you than the school-house, and if you will let Jessie come to me, instead of going to school, I will teach her to the best of my ability, and enjoy doing so. At any rate, while she is a little thing. You see, she would not have to come and go twice a day, in fact, she need hardly come every day—but we can arrange the details later, if you agree to it. Now think it over well, and we will talk about it again in a few days' time. And don't say 'no,' because you think it will be too much for me to do, for I should love to educate and train a little girl in the way *I* think she should be trained. It will be for me a most interesting experience. Now, Jessie, what do you say? Would you like to come to school with me?"

"Like it!" Neither Jessie nor her grandparents could find words to say how much they would like it, nor how grateful they were to Miss Barley; but at the same time they did feel it was too much for them to accept of her. Before, though, they had found words to express their feeling, or had stammered out half their thanks, the sound of the church bells came floating up across the fields, a signal to them all to part.

"I must fly," cried Miss Grace. "Do you think I can *run* through the lanes without shocking any one? I must go home before I go to church, or my sister will be quite alarmed," and away she hurried as fast as she could.

Patience had only time to carry in the tea-things, and leave them to wash on her return, for she had herself and Jessie to dress and get ready.

They were in time though, after all, for their feet kept pace with their happy thoughts and busy tongues, and there was no lingering on the way that evening.

CHAPTER V
HAPPY DAYS

Granp and granny did not hold out very long against Miss Grace Barley's plan, and in a short time all arrangements were made, and it was settled that Jessie was to go to Miss Barley's pretty house by the green every morning at ten, and to leave it at twelve, so that she might meet her grandfather as he went home to his dinner.

Thomas Dawson was head gardener at "The Grange," Sir Henry Weston's beautiful country-house, which lay a little distance beyond Springbrook station. Just outside the station were four cross-roads with a signpost in the middle of them to tell you where each one led. If you stood close to the signpost and faced the station, the road exactly behind you led down to Springbrook green and village, while the one on your right led along a wide flat road to "The Grange," and on, past that, through villages and towns until at last it reached the sea; and the road on your left led past "Sunnyside Cottage," and then on to Norton. This was the road that Jessie knew best, the one she had first walked with her grandfather on her way home that first evening.

From Miss Barley's house to the signpost was a very short distance, and here it was that Jessie and her grandfather were to meet every day and walk home together. Yet not every day, for Saturday, being a busy day for most people, was to be a whole holiday from lessons.

Miss Grace Barley had to gather flowers for the church and arrange them in the vases on Saturday mornings, and Miss Barley had extra things to do in the house and to go to Norton by train to do her shopping, and Jessie had to help her grandmother clean up the cottage and make all bright and neat for Sunday; so that it was nice and convenient for every one that Saturday should be a holiday from lessons.

On that first morning, when Jessie stood at Miss Barley's door and knocked, she felt very glad indeed to think that the day after to-morrow was Saturday and a whole holiday, for she felt very shy and rather frightened, and she longed to be back at home again with her granny and grandfather.

In fact, she was just edging towards the gate, with her mind almost made up to run home, when the door opened, and Miss Grace herself appeared. Miss Grace had on a hat and a large pair of gardening gloves, and in her hand she held a basket and the biggest pair of scissors Jessie had ever seen.

"Oh, Jessie!" she said, "you are just in time. I am going out to gather some flowers, and you will be able to help me. Come in, dear—no, we will not go in yet, we will go first and get the flowers, or the sun will be on them."

Jessie's frightened little face grew quite cheerful again. She thought this a delightful way of doing lessons, and marched along happily enough at Miss Grace's side, soon forgetting all her shyness in helping her to pick out the handsomest stocks and the finest roses. When the basket was full Miss Grace led the way to a window which opened down to the ground.

"This is my very own sitting-room," she said, as she stepped through the open window; "don't you think I ought to be very happy here?"

"Oh yes!" sighed Jessie, as she looked about her at the flowers, the pictures, and all the pretty things. "I shouldn't ever want to go away from it if it was mine."

Miss Grace laughed. "Well, we are going to do our lessons here, and perhaps when twelve o'clock comes you won't be the least little bit sorry to go away from it. But first of all I want you to help me arrange these flowers a little, and then go with me to carry them to a poor lady who is ill. Do you know the different kinds of roses by name, Jessie?"

Jessie did not. "Well, I will tell you some of them, and then you will be able to surprise grandfather. A gardener's granddaughter should know all these things. That lovely spray of little pink roses you are holding is called 'Dorothy Perkins.' You will remember that, won't you? And this deep orange-tinted bud is 'William Allen Richardson.'"

"'William Allen Richardson,'" repeated Jessie. "I think Miss Perkins is much prettier than Mr. Richardson."

Miss Grace laughed. "You are a very polite little girl, Jessie. Look at this one; this is called 'Homer,' but you need not call it Mr. or Mrs., but just plain 'Homer.'"

"I think it ought to be called 'pretty Homer,'" said Jessie, smiling.

By the time they had arranged all the flowers in the basket, she knew quite a lot about the different kinds and their names. Miss Grace made everything so attractive, and it was wonderful what a lot of interesting things she saw as she went about, even when she walked only across the green to Mrs. Parker's to leave the flowers.

Jessie did not see the poor dirty grey toad lying panting and frightened on the pathway, but Miss Grace did, and stooped and picked the poor thing up, and carrying it into her garden, placed it in a nice cool shady corner, underneath some bushes.

"Won't it bite you, or sting?" asked Jessie, her eyes wide with alarm, but Miss Grace reassured her. "That poor gentle little frightened thing hurt me!" she cried; "it could not if it wanted to, and I am sure it does not want to. It will help to take care of my flowers for me. You are not afraid to stroke it, Jessie, are you? Just look how fast its poor little heart is beating with fright! Isn't it cruel that any living creature should be as terrified as that!"

Jessie was ashamed for Miss Grace to know that she was almost as terrified of the toad as the toad was of her, so she stroked it, though very reluctantly, and the coldness of it made her jump so at first, that she thought she could never, never touch it again; but she tried not to be foolish, and she stroked its little head, and after that she did not mind it a bit, though she was glad Miss Grace did not ask her to carry it.

When they got back to the house they found two glasses of milk and a plate of biscuits in Miss Grace's room awaiting them, and after they had taken them, Miss Grace took down a book and read to Jessie, and Jessie, who already knew her letters and some of the easiest words, read a little to Miss Grace, and before she thought that half of the morning was gone, twelve o'clock had struck, and it was time to dress and run off to meet her grandfather at the four cross-roads.

When Jessie got to her place by the signpost, her grandfather was just coming along the road towards her. In his hand he held a big bunch of white roses and beautiful dark-green leaves. "Oh, how lovely!" gasped Jessie, when she caught sight of them.

"They'm 'Seven Sisters,'" said her grandfather; "they had overgrown the other things so much that I had to cut them back, and her ladyship told me to bring them home to you."

"Oh, thank you!" said Jessie delightedly. "What are the seven sisters called, granp? What is their real name? Of course they must have names."

Her grandfather did not understand her for the moment. "What are they called! Why, Rose, of course; but 'Seven Sisters' is what they're always known by."

"There couldn't be seven all called 'Rose,' could there?" asked Jessie gravely. "They *must* have a name each. Let me see, one could be 'White Rosie,' another 'Pink Rosie,' then there could be 'Red Rosie,' and 'Rosamund '; that's four."

"Perhaps the others is Cabbage Rosie, Dog Rosie, and Cider Rosie," said grandfather, chuckling.

Jessie burst into a peal of laughter as she thrust one hand into her grandfather's. "What things you do say, granp," she protested, and clasping her bouquet in her other hand, she skipped along by the old man's side. "Oh, I have learnt such a lot of things to-day," she said impressively. "There's one rose called 'Mr. Richardson,' another called 'Miss Perkins,' and another called 'Plain Homer,' and now there's 'Seven Sisters,' all with different names." Then she told him all about the toad, and the little story Miss Grace had read to her. "And to-morrow I am to learn to knit, and soon I'll be able to knit your stockings, granp, and cuffs to keep your arms warm in winter, and a shawl for granny."

"My!" exclaimed grandfather, with pleased surprise, "we shan't know ourselves, we shall be so warm and comfortable. But don't you go overworking yourself, little maid." Jessie laughed gleefully. She loved to think of all she was going to do for her grandfather and grandmother.

"Oh no," she said. "You see, I am very strong, and I like to have lots to do."

And "lots" she did do, in her staid, old-fashioned way. "I don't know whatever I should do without Jessie," granny would often remark to grandfather as the months went by, and Jessie became more and more useful about the house.

"It puzzles me to know how we ever got on before she came," grandfather would answer; and, as time went by, and Jessie grew taller and stronger and more and more capable, they wondered more and more frequently how they could ever have managed without her.

Jessie, too, often wondered how she had ever lived and been happy without her grandfather and grandmother, and "Sunnyside Cottage," and the garden, and the flowers, and her own rose-bush. At first she had thought a great deal about her mother, and wondered when she would come for her; and every nice new thing she had she wanted her to share, and every flower she had she wanted to save for her. But she saved them so often, and then had to throw them away dead, that at last she ceased to do so; and by and by, as the months passed, she grew accustomed to enjoying things without her mother; and at last she gave up wondering when she would come. In fact, for some time before she gave up expecting her, Jessie had begun to hope that when her mother did come, she would not want to take her away with her, but would live there always with herself, and granny, and granp.

Of her father's coming she never spoke but once, and that was when, with a frightened face, she said to her grandmother, "Granny, if father comes for me you won't let him take me away with him, will you?" And granny had reassured her with a sturdy—

"Why, bless your heart, child, your father isn't likely to want you, I can tell you, and he wouldn't dare to come here and show himself to me, I reckon; don't you be afraid, now, granny'll take care of you."

So Jessie tried not to be, and as the years went by, and nothing was heard from either of her parents, her fears lessened, though she could never think of her father without a shudder of dread lest he should some day come to take her away.

Three years had passed peacefully away, and Jessie was about eight years old when the next letter from Lizzie came to her parents.

Jessie never, to the end of her life, could forget the morning that letter reached them. It was a wet, dark November morning, and she had been lying awake for a long time listening to the patter-patter, swish-swish of the rain pouring against her window. She had heard her grandfather go down and open the front door as usual, and light the fire in the kitchen; then she heard him fill the kettle at the pump and put it on to boil. After that he went out again to open the hen-house door, and carry the hens their breakfast. She heard her grandmother go down the stairs, and a few moments later she heard heavy footsteps come splashing up the wet garden path, and very soon go down again.

Jessie got up and dressed herself, and made her way down. She had been singing to herself while she was dressing, so had not noticed anything unusual in the sounds and doings below stairs. But as she went down she did notice that the house seemed very quiet and still, and that there was no smell of breakfast cooking. Usually at this time her grandfather was busy in the scullery cleaning boots and knives, or doing some job or other, while her grandmother bustled back and forth, talking loudly, that her voice might reach above the frizzling of the frying-pan. But to-day there was a strange, most marked silence, broken only by the singing of the kettle, the plash of the rain outside, and a curious sound which Jessie could not make out, only she thought it sounded as though some one was in pain.

When she reached the foot of the stairs, she knew that she was right, and she stood and looked, with her heart sinking down, down, wondering with a great dread what could have happened. Her grandfather was sitting in his usual seat at the end of the table, holding a letter in his hand, while her grandmother stood beside him, her hand leaning heavily on his shoulder; and both their faces looked white and drawn, and full of trouble. Tears sprang to Jessie's eyes at sight of them. Neither was speaking, but every now and then there burst from the old man that strange sound that Jessie had heard, and it was like the cry of a hurt animal.

When she heard it again, and knew whence it came, Jessie flew to him in terror. "Oh, granp, what is it?" she cried. "Who has hurt him?" she cried, turning to her grandmother almost fiercely. "Who has done anything to granp—and you?" she added, when she caught sight of her grandmother's face.

Patience Dawson's hand slipped from her husband's shoulder down to Jessie's, and crept caressingly round the little girl's neck, while the old man threw his arm around her to draw her nearer to him.

"'Tis your mother, child," cried Patience, her words seeming to tumble from her anyhow. "She's dead! Our only child, and took from us for ever, and never knowing how much we loved and forgave her, and how we've hungered night and day for a sight of her—and now I shall never, never see her again!" and then poor Patience broke down, and kneeling beside her husband and grandchild, bowed her head on the table and wept uncontrollably.

At the sight of their trouble Jessie's own tears fell fast. "Mother," she cried, scarcely grasping the real state of the case, and all it meant to her. "Mother! dead? Granp, mother isn't really dead, is she? Won't I—won't I never see her any more," the truth gradually forcing itself on her mind— "won't she ever come and live here with us, and see my rose—and—and all the things I've been saving for her?" Her little face was white now, and her lips quivering with the pain of realization.

Her grandfather shook his head. "She won't ever come to us; never, never no more," he sighed heavily. "But maybe," he added a moment later, speaking slowly and with difficulty, "maybe she sees and knows now, better than she has all these years—and is happier."

"Why didn't she write, why didn't she tell us where she was?" wailed Patience despairingly. "I would have wrote at once and told her how we'd forgiven everything."

"Poor maid," said Thomas Dawson softly, "I reckon she had her reasons; her letter tells us that, without putting it into so many words. Read it again, mother, read it to the child—I can't."

Patience took up the letter, but it was some time before she could control herself sufficiently to begin.

"My dearest Father and Mother,

> "This is to tell you I am very ill, dying. The doctor says
> that if I want to let any one know, I must do so at once. You
> are the only ones that care, and I am writing to you to say
> good-bye for ever. I have always hoped that some day I
> should see you again, and my dear home, and my dearest,
> dearest child. I am sure you will forgive me the wrong
> I did, and my cruel behaviour. I couldn't die happy if I
> didn't feel sure of that; but, dear father and mother, I know
> your loving hearts. No words can tell how I've pined and
> longed for my little Jessie, my own little baby, all these
> years. At first I thought I should have died for want of her,
> but I knew she was happy—that was my only comfort—
> and I could not have found clothes nor food for her. I was
> going to write to you as soon as we were settled, but Harry
> lost that situation almost at once, and since then we have
> been on the tramp and never had a home. It has been a
> cruel life, and I have often thanked God on my knees that
> my darling was spared it. I know you love her and have
> taken care of her. Don't let her forget me, dear father and
> mother, and don't ever let her go from you. She is yours—I
> give her to you, and I thank you with all my heart for all
> you've done for her. Give her my love—oh, that I could
> kiss her dear little face again! Good-bye, dear father and

mother, I can never forgive myself for all the misery I have caused you; but I know you will forgive me, and believe I loved you all the time. The woman here is kind to me, and she has promised to keep this letter safe, and send it to you when I am gone. Good-bye."

"Your loving daughter,"
"Lizzie."

The letter, which had been placed in an envelope and directed by Lizzie's own hand, came in a larger envelope, and with it a slip of paper on which was written in a good firm hand, "Your poor daughter died this morning. Yours truly, Mary Smith."

The letter bore the Birmingham postmark, but no other clue.

"We don't even know where she died," sobbed Thomas, "that I may go and bring her home to bury her," and this thought hurt the poor old man cruelly.

"If you did know, he probably wouldn't let you have her poor body, not if he thought you wanted it," cried Patience bitterly. She could not bring herself to mention her son-in-law by name. "He would hurry her into her grave rather than she should come back to us," and then she burst into bitter weeping again.

CHAPTER VI
TAKEN BY SURPRISE

After that first outburst of grief, Thomas Dawson did not speak much of his trouble, but it was none the less deep for that. In fact, it was so deep, and the wound was such a cruel one, it was almost more than he could bear.

The thought of his dead daughter never left him. Through the day, when he was at work, through the long evenings when he sat silent and sad, gazing into the fire, and through the nights when he lay sleepless, he brooded over the wrongs his daughter's husband had done them all, and was full of remorse for his own hard-heartedness—as he called it now—in not having forgiven her at once when she ran away from her home. And more than all was he haunted by the thought of her lonely death after her cruelly hard life. He pictured her lying in her pauper's grave in an unknown burial-ground, away amongst strangers, unknown, uncared for, unremembered, and these thoughts aged him fast.

Jessie was too young to notice it, but those older saw how he began to stoop, how his feet lagged as he walked, how the colour had faded from his hair and from the bright blue eyes, which had been such a noticeable feature of his face. All the life and fun had gone out of him too; even Jessie could not rouse him.

Patience bore her grief in another way, it was merged to some extent in her anxiety about her husband. With regard to Lizzie she felt less anxiety and pain about her now than she had done when Lizzie had been alive, and living a miserable life with the weak, ne'er-do-well husband who had been the ruin of her happiness and theirs. Trouble left its mark on Patience too, she became gentler and quieter, she seemed to lose some of her strength and spirit, and to lean more and more on her little granddaughter. And Jessie, pleased and proud to be useful, and trusted and able to help, turned to with a will, and by degrees took a great deal on her young shoulders.

She still went to Miss Grace Barley to be taught, for the hours suited them all well, and though her grandmother protested often that it was too much for Miss Grace to do, and declared that Jessie must go to the school along with the others, Miss Grace begged to be allowed to keep her.

"Jessie can repay me by coming and being our maid by and by," she said laughingly—"that is if she wants to go out into service, and you can spare her, Mrs. Dawson."

"I shall have to some day," said Mrs. Dawson, with a sigh and a smile; "she will have to support herself, of course, when she grows up, and it's our duty to see she has the training."

So it became the dream of Jessie's life to be Miss Barley's maid, to live in the "White Cottage," and have the joy and honour of keeping it in the beautiful order in which she had always seen it.

It had been a curious, uncommon education that the child had had, but the results were certainly satisfactory. She could darn and sew beautifully, make and mend, knit and patch, and read and write, cook a little, and do all manner of housework, while she was quite clever in her knowledge of flowers and their ways.

Every Saturday morning she devoted herself to helping her grandmother clean the cottage and prepare for Sunday. It was her task to polish all the knives and forks, to dust the bedrooms and the kitchen. Her grandmother would not let her do the harder work, such as scrubbing the floors or tables, though Jessie often longed to try; but while granny was busy washing the floors, it was Jessie's great delight to mount on a chair and clean the little lattice windows of the kitchen and parlour.

When she was about ten years old her other longings were unexpectedly realized, and the scrubbing fell to her to do too, for one chill autumn morning Mrs. Dawson found herself too unwell to get up. She had been ailing for a week or two. "'Tis the damp and cold got into my bones," she had said, making light of it, "and they'll just have to get out again, that's all. There is nothing like moving about for working it off. If I'd sat still as some folks do, I shouldn't be able to move at all by this time."

But on this morning even she was forced to give in. "I think the cold has touched my liver," she said feebly, "and I don't feel fit for nothing. I'll stay in bed for a bit, that's the best way," and indeed she felt far too unwell to do anything else. Thomas called at the doctor's house on his way to work, and came home early to dinner to hear his report.

"He says it's the yellow jaunders," said Jessie, in an awed voice, looking very grave and alarmed, "and he says I must not be frightened if granny turns orange colour. Do you think she has been eating too many oranges, granp? She had two on Sunday—big ones!"

Granp smiled, in spite of his anxiety. He knew that an attack of jaundice was no trifling illness for a woman of Patience's age, and the next day he did not go to work, but waited to see the doctor himself.

The news in the morning, though, was slightly better, and although Mrs. Dawson had to keep her bed for some time, their greatest anxiety was lifted, and their spirits grew higher and more hopeful.

Jessie now was in her element. She swept and dusted, scrubbed and polished, waited on her grandmother and took care of her grandfather like any little old woman. All day long her busy feet and hands were going, never seeming to tire; and in her joy at seeing her grandmother getting well again, and her grandfather more happy, and in her pleasure in taking care of them both, her spirits kept as bright and gay, and her laugh as infectious and joyous as it was possible for any one's to be.

So things were when that Saturday dawned which, undreamed of, was to change everything for all of them.

It was a fresh bright autumn day, with the sun shining cheerfully, but with just that touch of cold in the air which makes one realize that summer is past and winter not so very far off. In the garden the chrysanthemums were covered with a fine show of buds, and Jessie looked at them eagerly to see if any would be out on the morrow, for the doctor had said that Mrs. Dawson might get up for a little while on Sunday and come down-stairs.

The news put them all in a great bustle. Jessie felt that all her credit depended on everything, indoors and out, being just a little cleaner and trimmer and more orderly than if her grandmother had been about herself. Things had to be got from Norton too, so grandfather took the train thither to do the shopping, and Jessie was left to sweep and scrub and polish to her heart's content. She and granp were up early on that important morning—indeed, there was little likelihood of any one's oversleeping on that day, and so well did they work that by the time Jessie went up to know what her grandmother would like for dinner, the greater part of their tasks were done and grandfather had already started for Norton.

"I don't want anything but a cup of tea and a piece of toast now," said her grandmother in answer to Jessie's question.

"Won't you have some of the jelly Miss Barley brought you?"

"No, child. I feel much more inclined for a cup of tea. If you've got any fire in I'd like a slice of toast, but if you haven't I'll have a piece of dry bread.

I dare say you'd like one of the little apple pasties Mrs. Maddock brought over."

Mrs. Maddock was the wife of the farmer who lived a little way from them, along the road to the four turnings.

"Yes, I would," said Jessie, "I am hungry."

"I don't wonder," said her grandmother, smiling, "working as you have been. Why, there won't be anything left for me to do when I get up. Is the kettle nearly boiling?"

"Yes," said Jessie, "it is singing. I'll have to step over to Mrs. Maddock's for the milk, and by the time I come back it will be ready. Will you be all right, granny, while I'm gone? I won't be away more than five minutes."

"Yes, I shall be all right, child; I'll promise not to run away, and I don't suppose any burglar will break in here," she laughed gently.

"Well, I could soon catch you, if you did," laughed Jessie, "but I don't know about a burglar, I would have to run to Mrs. Maddock's again and borrow their dog. Good-bye, granny."

"Put on your hat and coat," granny called after her.

"Oh, need I?" asked Jessie, with just a shade of impatience in her voice.

"Why, yes, child, it is quite chilly, and you have been so hot over your work."

So Jessie stayed a moment in the kitchen to put on her hat and coat—and oh, how glad she was of it before that night was ended—and taking her milk-can in one hand and a penny in the other, away she ran down the garden and out into the road. She stood for a moment and glanced along the road in each direction, just to make sure that there was no one near who would be likely to knock and disturb her grandmother before she got back again, but there was not a living creature in sight, that she could see, so on she ran to the farm. Mrs. Maddock kept her a minute or two to inquire after Mrs. Dawson, and to give her a flower to wear to church the next day, then Jessie hurried away again as fast as her full milk-can would allow her.

The side entrance to the farm, to which Jessie had to go, was a few hundred yards down a lane which branched off the main road. When she came out and down this lane again, a man was standing at the end of it where it emerged on to the high road. He was standing looking down the lane very eagerly at first, but, as Jessie drew nearer, he stepped back a pace or two, and looked nervously first over one shoulder and then over the other, along the high road.

Jessie was ten years old, and accustomed to seeing strange rough-looking men about, so that there seemed no reason why she should feel frightened, but she did, and for a moment almost turned and ran back to the friendly shelter of Mrs. Maddock's dairy. Later on she often wished she had, but then, as she told herself, he would probably have run after her and caught her.

With her heart beating very fast, but trying to look quite calm and unconcerned, she walked sturdily on. As soon as she had got past him, she thought, and had turned the corner, she would race home as fast as her legs could carry her, and if she did spill some milk granny would forgive her when she knew how frightened she had been. But the man evidently did not intend that she should pass him, for as she drew near he stood right in her path, and to prevent any chance of escape he seized her by the wrist.

"I've been looking for you, this long while," he said roughly. "Now don't make a noise," as Jessie screamed "help." "If you're quiet I shan't hurt you, but if you make a noise and bring a crowd round, I'll thrash you to within an inch of your life. Do you hear?"

"Let me go," wailed Jessie, struggling to release her wrist.

"I must go home, granny's waiting for me, she is ill."

"And I've been waiting for you longer than 'granny' has. I've been waiting hours. Your grandfather's gone away, isn't he?"

"Yes, to Norton."

"That's all right."

"He'll be home soon," retorted Jessie, in the vain hope of frightening the man. "Oh, do let me go, please! granny is ill, and waiting for me to take her her dinner."

"I've waited longer for my dinner than ever she has. You shall bring me mine instead. In bed, is she?"

"Yes," sobbed Jessie.

"That's all right."

"Oh, would no one ever come," Jessie wondered, looking frantically about her.

The man read her thoughts and actions. "No, it isn't likely there'll be anybody about just yet, they are all to market, or off somewhere. I took care to choose my time well. Is your grandfather coming home by train?"

"Yes," sobbed Jessie. "Oh, *please* let me go. What do you want? I haven't got any money—"

"It's *you* I want, yourself, Jessie Lang."

Jessie looked up in surprise, wondering how he knew her name. She had thought him a tramp only, though a particularly horrible one. Now a deeper fear crept into her heart, causing her to feel sick and faint with alarm, and a dread of she hardly knew what.

"Why do you want me?" she gasped, trembling, scarcely able to form her words, so furiously was her poor little heart beating.

"Why do I want you? 'Cause I'm your own father, and I've been robbed of you for five years! Natural enough, isn't it, that a man should want his own child to come and look after him?"

"But I've got to look after granny and granp," gasped Jessie, "they are old, and granny's ill, and—and they've taken care of me all this time, and now I've got to take care of them. I'm very sorry, but I can't look after you too."

"Dear me!" muttered the man. "How polite we are! But whether you can or you can't, you've got to! I think it's a pity they haven't brought you up better, and taught you your duty to your father. Well, I can't be wasting any more time here. We've got a long journey before us."

"Oh no, no!" cried Jessie, beside herself with dismay; "don't take me away!—*please*, please don't make me leave granny!"

"Shut up that noise," interrupted her father roughly. "You've got to learn that I never stand whining and bellowing; and the sooner you learn it the better. Now I did mean to spare you all the trouble of saying 'good-bye,' but on second thoughts I'll go in and explain a bit to the old woman, so hurry along and lead the way. I don't want any nonsense about putting the police on my track to find you and bring you back, so it shall be all open and straight. You are mine by law, and I am going to stick to the law."

Jessie was trembling so, she could scarcely drag her limbs along, but she did her best to obey her father's command, a wild hope springing up in her heart that if once she got within the shelter of home and granny, all would be well.

As she opened the cottage door she heard her grandmother's voice calling down to her. "Why, Jessie, wherever have you been? I was afraid something had happened. The kettle has boiled over and over until the fire must be nearly put out." But she had scarcely finished speaking before Jessie dashed up the stairs and into her room breathless, almost speechless, her face white, and with a look on it that haunted Patience Dawson for many a long day.

"Oh, granny, he's come, father's come, and he's going to take me away! Oh, granny, what shall I do! Save me! save me! don't let him have me! I'm afraid of him!"

But before Mrs. Dawson, in her utter bewilderment and fright, could take in what it all meant, heavy footsteps mounted the stairs quickly, and she saw Harry Lang, the man she so detested and dreaded, standing in the doorway.

"Don't make that row," he shouted roughly to the child, "nice way that to carry on when your dear grandmother is ill! Do you want to make her worse! Be quiet, can't you, and be quick. I've got no time to waste."

Jessie subsided into silence, a little moan alone escaping her as she clung to her grandmother.

"It's simple enough," he went on, turning to Mrs. Dawson, "I want my daughter, and I've come to fetch her. You've had her for five years, and now I want her for five—or fifteen, or fifty," he added, "just as it suits me."

"You can't—you've no right—you deserted her. She is ours."

"That's just where you make a mistake, old lady," he sneered, his face lighting up with an ugly mocking smile. "She is mine, not yours, and I've every right to her. I didn't desert her, and you can't prove I did, and I guess if we went to law about it, it would be you that would be in the dock for stealing her, or receiving stolen goods, so to speak, from her mother, who stole her."

"You knew where she was!" gasped Mrs. Dawson, stunned by this new aspect of affairs. "You knew poor Lizzie had sent her here—you know you did."

"Prove it," he said tauntingly. "That's all! Prove it!" Then suddenly remembering that time was flying, he changed his tone. "Well, anyhow, you can settle all that to your liking later on, I can't stay to argue now. I've married again, and my wife keeps a lodging-house, and wants some one to help her, some one strong and healthy, like Jessie here, and I've come for her. I didn't see the fun of paying a girl, when we could get a better one for nothing; and I came for her to-day because I thought it would be nice and quiet, not too many about, and not too many leave-takings. Now, Jess, say good-bye to your granny, I want to be off before the old man gets back, so as to spare him the pain," with a cruel laugh.

Was there no one to help them! No one to appeal to! Jessie and her grandmother looked at each other despairingly. They could think of no one within a mile or two, except Mrs. Maddock and her little maid, and how could they reach them, and what could they do to help if they did! A deep, hopeless despair settled on both of them.

"If you've anything you wants to bring along with you," said her father curtly, "look sharp and get it. I don't s'pose it's more than I can carry."

Jessie was too stunned to know quite what she was doing. In her room she had a big old-fashioned carpet bag that her grandfather had once given her because she so admired the flowers on its sides, and into this she thrust some of her clothes without in the least realizing what she was doing. When, though, she came to her little shelf of books, to a box Miss Grace had given her, a work-basket her grandfather and grandmother had bought her on her birthday, and a picture which had been Miss Barley's present, she stayed her hand. She would not take any of her treasures to be knocked about perhaps in a busy lodging-house. She would leave them here, they would seem like a link between her and home—for no other place would ever be "home" to her, she knew.

She took her little Prayer-book, the one that had been her mother's, granny had given it to her on her eighth birthday, and she treasured it dearly; it had her mother's name and her own written in it, and that seemed always to draw them nearer and form a little link between.

It was all soon over, and Jessie, without daring to look around her beloved little room again, crept away back to her granny, her eyes blinded with tears.

"Granny, you'll 'tend to my rose for me, won't you," she whispered in a choked voice, "till I come home again, and—and kiss granp for me, and—oh, granny, granny, what shall I do, I can't go away! I can't! I can't! I think I shall die if—"

Perhaps mercifully, her father cut the leave-taking short. No good could be done, not a fraction of their misery lessened by prolonging it, and before Jessie had finished sobbing out her last words, he had picked her up and carried her down-stairs and out of the house.

"This way," he said, when he put her down in the road. "I like seclusion when I take a walk. There's a station I prefer to Springbrook, it's one I used to favour a good bit," with a meaning little laugh, "and if I haven't forgot my way all these years, and they haven't altered the face of the country, the shortest cut to it lies through these very fields, so step out and put your best foot foremost."

CHAPTER VII
THE JOURNEY AND THE ARRIVAL

Harry Lang's "short cut" to the next station meant a good two hours of heavy walking, sometimes over rough uneven ground, sometimes through a little coppice, or along a quiet lane, all of them unknown to Jessie. For this very reason, perhaps, the way seemed even longer than it really was, but to the poor exhausted child it seemed endless. Her head ached distractingly, her back and legs ached, and her feet had almost refused to do her bidding long before she reached the station.

Her father noticed that she lagged, but it never occurred to him that the real reason was that she was exhausted—at least it did not occur to him until, when they at last reached the refreshment room, Jessie dropped like a stone upon the floor.

"What are you doing?" he snapped crossly, "get up! Can't you see where you are going?"

But Jessie neither saw, nor heard, nor moved. The kindly-faced woman behind the counter first leaned out over it to look at her, then came around.

"Why, she's in a dead faint," she cried, lifting the limp little hand; "has she walked far? She looks dead beat."

Harry Lang muttered something about "just a mile or so," but he did not enlarge on the subject, and he seemed so morose and surly that no one felt drawn to say more to him than they could help. The woman lifted Jessie up, and laid her gently on a couch, but she had bathed her brow and her hands, and held smelling-salts under her nose for quite a long while before she showed any signs of life, and Harry Lang had wished himself miles away, and regretted his day's work many times before Jessie with a deep, deep sigh at last opened her eyes.

For a moment she looked about her uncomprehendingly; then, as realization came to her, the woman bending over her heard her moan despairingly.

"Is she ill?" she asked.

"No," said Harry Lang curtly, "only a bit tired and upset at having to leave the folks that brought her up. Maybe she's hungry; we've walked a good step to get here, and we haven't had a bite of anything. I'm hungry myself, so I dare say she is. Hungry, Jessie?"

"I want to go home, I must—I must. Oh, let me go," moaned Jessie wildly, looking up at him beseechingly; but at sight of his face she shrank back frightened, and the words died on her lips.

"You are going home as fast as I can take you," he said roughly; "if you'd sent word, I dare say they'd have got a special," he added, with a sarcastic laugh.

"I'll give her something to eat," said the woman, without a smile at his joke. "I dare say she'll feel better then. She looks to me dead beat," and she laid Jessie gently back, and went behind the counter and poured her out a basin of soup from some that was being kept hot there. To Jessie, who had had no food since breakfast-time, the soup brought new life. She took it all, and a large slice of bread with it, to the great satisfaction of her new friend, who watched delightedly the colour coming back to the poor little white face.

"Where do you want to get to, to-night?" she asked, turning to Harry Lang.

"London."

"Um! The next train that stops here doesn't come in till 10.15. It is a long time for her to wait, and late for her to get home."

"'Tisn't going to kill her," answered Jessie's father shortly. "Everybody has got something to put up with sometimes. She is lucky not to have to walk all the way." He hated to be asked questions, and grew cross at being obliged to answer them.

"It's my opinion she'd never reach the other end if she had to do that," said the woman curtly. Then, turning to Jessie, she said gently, "If you lie back again, dear, maybe you'll be able to sleep, and that will rest you, and help to pass the time too."

Jessie, only too glad to obey, and not to have to move her aching body again, nestled back on the hard cushions, and turning her face away from the light, shut her eyes, and soon was miles away from her present surroundings and her miseries, in a deep dreamless sleep, and she knew nothing more until she was wakened suddenly by a tremendous rumbling and shaking, puffing and roaring, close at hand, which made her start up in a terrible panic of alarm.

For a moment she did not realize where she was or what had happened; her brain was dazed, her eyes full of sleep. Then her father came in, and seizing her by the arm hurried her out of the room and across the platform to the brightly-lighted train drawn up there. He gave her no time for farewells to the kind-hearted woman who had helped her so much, nor did he thank her himself. Poor Jessie could only look back over her shoulder and try to thank her with her eyes and smiles.

"Thank you very much," she called out, her voice sounding very weak and small in the midst of all the uproar; but the gratitude on her face and in her eyes spoke more than words.

"I've thought dozens of times of that poor little child," the woman remarked next day to one of the porters; "the man looked so cruel and horrid, and the child so frightened. I should like to know the truth about them. I am sure he was unkind to her."

Once inside the railway carriage, Jessie's father put her to sit in the corner by the window, and seated himself next to her. He was so anxious that no one should speak to her that he even gave up the comfortable corner seat himself, and sat bolt upright beside her, a bit of self-denial which did not improve his temper, which was at no time a sweet one; and when at last Waterloo was reached, it was with no gentle hand that he shook and roused her from the kindly sleep which had fallen on her again, and blotted for the time all her woes from her memory.

With a shock Jessie started to her feet, staring about her with wide, dazed, sleep-filled eyes. "Wake up, can't you? I can't stay here all night while you has your sleep out!"

No one else ever spoke to her in that tone and manner. In a moment poor Jessie's eyes and brain were as wide awake and alert as fear could force them. That dreaded voice would rouse her from the sleep of death almost, she thought. Shaking with cold and dread, she followed him along the lighted platform, and out into the gloom and squalor of the streets.

A heavy rain was coming down in sheets, driven in their faces by a cold, gusty wind. It hit the pavement and splashed up against her cold little legs and ankles until they were soaked through; it beat on her face until she was nearly blinded; and, bewildered by the bright lights, and the deep shadows, and the glitter of the wet streets in the light of the lamps, she would soon have been lost indeed, had her father not caught her by the hand.

On they went, and on and on, an endless distance it seemed to Jessie. Her father never once spoke to her, and she was afraid to speak to him. At last, though, she summoned up courage. "Where are we going, father?"

"Home."

"Are we nearly there?"

"You'll know in time, so hold your noise."

She "held her noise." At least she did not venture to speak again, and "in time" she did know, but it was a long time first.

Jessie had long been too tired to notice anything that was passing, and when at last they did stop before a house, and went up to the door of it, she was too exhausted to notice the place or the house, or anything about her. She wanted only to be allowed to lie down somewhere, anywhere, and not have to move, or speak, or even think.

When the door was at last opened she saw before her what looked like a black pit, and that was all. Her father must have been able to see more than she, for he swore at some one for keeping him waiting so long, and Jessie supposed it was at an unseen person who had opened the door to them, then he walked quickly ahead, telling Jessie to follow him.

Follow him! How could she, when she could see nothing and did not know where her next step would land her? She did not dare, though, do anything but obey, so, groping blindly, and sliding her feet carefully before her, one at a time, she crept with all the speed she could in direction in which she thought he had gone.

"Mind the stairs," said some one behind her, and at the same moment Jessie's foot went over the top one.

"Harry, you might have helped the child down," said the voice behind her, more tartly, and Jessie guessed it was the door-opener who spoke, and who was following her. Harry Lang muttered something surlily enough, but he did pick up a lamp from somewhere, and held it out for her to see the rest of her way by, and Jessie clambered down the remaining stairs in comparative comfort.

"You'd better give the kid something to eat, and pack her off to bed as soon as you can," he said. "She's pretty well fagged out, and so am I," he added.

Jessie looked round to see to whom he was speaking, and saw standing in the doorway a little thin woman, with a sharp, cross face, and dull, tired eyes, eyes which looked as though they never brightened, or lost their look of weary hopelessness. This was her stepmother. She gave no sign of welcome, no word of comfort to the child, yet, somehow, Jessie's heart went out to her a little. It might have been only that in her terror of her father, she was ready to cling to any one who might stand between her and him.

"There's bread and butter —"

"Bread and butter!" roared her husband, "is that all? Do you mean to say you haven't got anything hot and tasty for me after all I've been through to get this brat here, for nothing in the world but to help you to do nothing all day long —"

"There's plenty for you," she retorted coldly. "I was speaking of the child. I knew you wouldn't want to share yours with her," and Harry Lang, who had stepped threateningly towards her, drew back again, looking rather foolish and very cross. "Where is it?" he snapped.

"In the oven," and she took out a big covered basin and put before him.

Whatever the contents might have been, they smelt very savoury and seemed to please him, but he never offered a mouthful of it to his famishing little daughter, as she stood by, looking at him. A thick slice of bad bread with some butter spread thinly on it was Jessie's fare, and she wished the butter had been omitted altogether, so horrid did it smell and taste.

As soon as he had finished the last mouthful of his supper Harry Lang got up, and without a word to either of them, slouched out of the kitchen and up-stairs to bed. Mrs. Lang began at once to clear a very large old sofa of its untidiness.

"You'll have to sleep here," she said; "the house is so full there isn't room for you anywhere else. Make haste and get your things off. I want to get to bed myself. I've got to be up at five, and it's past one now."

Jessie looked with dismay at the collection of dirty-looking shawls and coats her stepmother was piling on the sofa as "bedclothes," and if she had not been so dead tired, she could never have brought herself to lie down under them. Visions of her own sweet little room and spotless bed rose before her, and overcame her control.

"Is this your bag?"

"Yes," said Jessie tearfully, a sob rising in her throat.

The woman looked at her with dull interest. "You'd better keep your feelings to yourself," she said; "there's no time for any here. Try to go to sleep, and don't think about anything," she added, not unkindly. "You are overtired to-night, you'll feel better to-morrow." She helped Jessie into her rough bed, and tucked the shawl about her, but she did not kiss her. "Now make haste and go to sleep," she said, "for I shall be down very early, and then you'll have to get up," and she walked away, taking the lamp with her.

Jessie shut her eyes and tried to go to sleep, but her nerves were all unstrung, brain and ears were all on the alert, and there seemed to be curious, unaccountable sounds on all sides of her. She had not been alone more than a minute or two before there were strange scraping noises in the kitchen not far from her. "Mice!" thought Jessie, "or beetles."

She was a fairly brave child, but she had a perfect horror of black beetles, and her heart sank at the thought of them. She drew the shawl over her head as well as she could, and wrapped up her arms in it, but still she felt that the beetles were running, running everywhere, over the walls and over her, and she could scarcely refrain from shrieking aloud in her horror. Then came louder and more dreadful sounds, the cries of people quarrelling; they seemed to be in the very house too; Jessie uncovered her head to hear, then covered it quickly again, sick and faint with fear. A drunken man reeled past the house, singing noisily; to Jessie in the kitchen area he seemed horribly near.

She grew more and more frightened with each sound she heard. She was alone in the dark, with dreadful things happening all around her, in a house that she did not even know her way about. She felt sick and faint with terror and horror of the place, and longing for home and all that she had lost.

Then she remembered suddenly that she had not said her prayers. It had all seemed so strange, and her stepmother had hurried her so, that she had never thought of it until now.

"Oh, I can't get out and kneel down," she thought. "I might step on some beetles. I am sure if God sees how dreadful everything is, and how frightened I am, that He will forgive me if I say them here. And she began—

> "I trust myself, dear God, to Thee,
> Keep every evil far from me.

"Does that mean drunken men and beetles," she wondered feverishly, "'I trust myself, dear God, to Thee;' if I do, He will take care of me, for certain," and a ray of comfort crept into her poor little aching heart. "Granp told me so." And for the first time in her life Jessie felt the true meaning of the dear old grandfather's lessons in the garden, or by the kitchen fire.

Hitherto she had been sheltered and loved and guarded, been well clothed, and fed, and cared for. Now, for the first time, she felt the need of some one to turn to, and her prayers meant more than they had ever meant before. They came from her heart, and were real petitions.

"Granp said God loved little children, and always listened to them," and with this comforting thought she at last fell asleep.

CHAPTER VIII
THE NEW HOME

It seemed to Jessie that she was still saying, "Keep every evil far from me," and trying to go to sleep, when a voice said sharply—

"Now then, it's time to wake up! Make haste and get your clothes on, for your father and one of the lodgers will be here wanting their breakfasts presently."

Jessie woke with a great start, and sprang up, struggling with the shawl which was still wrapped about her head. Free of this, she looked about her in a dazed way, trying to rouse herself and collect her wits. It was not yet daylight, of course, and the lighted lamp stood on the table in the midst of the dirty dishes just as it had the night before; her stepmother too—her hair and dress and whole appearance were exactly as they had been the night before, the only difference being that she seemed, if anything, less agreeable.

"Wake up! wake up!" she called sharply again. "I want you to make yourself useful, not to be giving me more trouble. Get on your things, then light the fire as quick as you can—no, I'll light the fire to-day, because your father can't bear to be kept waiting, but I shall look to you to do it other mornings, and to get up without being called, too."

"Yes," said Jessie dutifully, "I hope I shall be able to wake up." She was so sleepy at the moment that she could scarcely stand, or see to get into her garments. She looked around her for a place where she could wash. Cold water would help her to wake up, perhaps. It was really painful to be so terribly sleepy.

"Please, where can I wash?" she asked at last. "I—I can't wake—up; I—I—" and she was asleep again. Her stepmother's sharp voice soon roused her, though.

"A place to wash in!" she snapped crossly. "Why, you must wait until some of them have gone out, then you can go to one of the bedrooms, unless you'd like to wash at the tap, out there," pointing to the scullery; "there's a dipper there you can use."

Jessie gladly accepted the last offer. She was longing to feel the freshness of cold water on her aching head and heavy eyes, and her hot face, and she groped her way out to the scullery.

It was lighted by a candle only, but even so Jessie could see the untidy muddle of everything. The sink by the tap was crowded with pots and pans and dirty dishes, and so was the table and the dirty floor. Where was she to wash, and where was the dipper? She looked around her hopelessly. She was so heavy with sleep she could hardly see, so aching in every limb she could scarcely stand; and the sight of the miserable place, and the close smell of it, made her feel positively sick and ill.

She did not dare, though, trouble her stepmother any further, she had to act for herself; so she looked about her, first of all for the dipper, and presently saw it standing, full of potato peelings, on the floor under the sink. She seized it thankfully, and emptying its contents on to a dirty plate, went to the tap and gave it a good wash out. While she was doing this her eye fell on a piece of soap. At last she managed to draw a dipperful of clean fresh water, and glad enough she was; it felt so delicious, in fact, and she enjoyed it so much, she could not bear to tear herself away from it, until her mother's sharp voice brought her back to her duties again, and the rest of her toilet was finished more hurriedly.

"What shall I do first?" she asked timidly, when she was ready. In her clean pinafore, with her hair well brushed, and her cheeks still glowing from the cold water, she looked so fresh and such a pleasant sight to see, that a ray of something like pleased surprise showed itself for a moment even on Mrs. Lang's tired face.

"Can you wash up two or three of the cups and things without smashing them?" she asked.

"Oh yes," said Jessie, almost reproachfully, "I always do at home." But the mere mention of that name brought the tears to her eyes, and prevented her saying more.

"Well, do that first. You needn't wash more than two cups and plates. I'd better lend you something to put on over your clean apron, or you'll be wanting another before the day is out."

"I've got my overalls here," said Jessie, with pride. "Granny made me two," and she stepped to the old bag and lifted out a dark-blue galateen pinafore which covered her all up to the hem of her frock.

When she came back from washing the dishes she brought the sweeping-brush with her, and, as a matter of course, began to sweep up the littered floor. Mrs. Lang opened her mouth to tell her to stop, then apparently thought better of it, and let her go on. The kitchen swept, Jessie asked for a duster to dust the chairs and other things, which needed it badly enough!

"A duster! Don't bother me about such things. We haven't got any."

Jessie looked nonplussed. "May I have this?" she asked at last, picking up a bit of rag from a pile of things untidily heaped on a chair. Mrs. Lang, though, was gone, and did not hear her. Jessie looked at the rag, and pondered. At last, however, the temptation to wipe off some of the dust became too much for her, and she used it. "I can wash out the rag again," she comforted herself by thinking. "I wonder what I had better do next," for Mrs. Lang had not returned. "I s'pose I'd better sweep out the passage and brush down the steps. Oh, I do want some breakfast!" she added, with a sigh.

While she was sweeping down the steps before the front door, her stepmother came into the kitchen again. The semblance of a smile crossed her face as she looked at the neatly-arranged chairs, and heard the broom going in the distance.

"We're to be kept tidy, now, I s'pose," she muttered, with a laugh. "I wonder how long it'll last. She won't get much encouragement here."

Jessie came into the kitchen with her broom, and found her stepmother frying bacon. It smelt very good, and Jessie was ravenously hungry.

"Does father have to go to work every day as early as this?" she asked.

"Work!" cried Mrs. Lang, with a scornful laugh. "Work! I've never known your father work since he crossed my path! It's the races he's off to; you wouldn't find him get up at this hour for anything else."

Jessie stared wide-eyed. "Doesn't he ever work?" she gasped. "How does he live, then?"

"Well you may ask!" snapped Mrs. Lang bitterly. "He's kept. I do the work, and he finds that more to his taste. I've got the house full of lodgers, and I can tell you it takes me all my time, and more, to look after them. I never get any pleasure, and your father never gets any work, and he thinks that is just as it should be."

Jessie stood for a moment looking very thoughtful. Everything in this house seemed to her wrong. Just as it all used to be in her old home before she went to her grandfather's; but she knew nothing better then, she was too young. Now she was older and better able to understand, for she had had a long and happy experience of what a home could and should be, where each did a share, and thought always of others first. She felt suddenly a great pity for her stepmother, and a liking such as she had not thought possible an hour or so ago. Perhaps she could do something, she thought, to make her less unhappy; at any rate she could help her.

"I will help you," she said, looking up at her with a smile.

"It won't be so hard with two of us to see to things."

Mrs. Lang's face softened a little, and a smile actually gleamed in her eyes as she glanced from the frying-pan to Jessie. "Yes, you can help a bit, I expect, you seem to know how to set about things. Did you help your grandmother?"

"Oh yes, a lot," said Jessie, and at the recollection the tears brimmed up in her eyes. "I wonder how she is, and how granp is! Oh, I expect he was in a dreadful way when he came home, and heard what had happened!" and at the thought poor Jessie's tears overflowed, and she sobbed bitterly.

"Hush, don't make that noise," said her stepmother quickly, but not unkindly. "Be quiet, child, your father's coming, and he'll beat you if you go on like that. Oh, it's you, Tom," as a young man lounged heavily into the kitchen, "I thought 'twas Harry."

Tom Salter dropped into a chair by the table with a tired yawn. "Yes, it's me; I'm up, but I ain't awake," he said, with a laugh. "Hullo," as he caught sight of Jessie, "is this the little girl you was telling me about?"

"Yes, this is Jessie."

He looked at Jessie and smiled, and she smiled back. He had a good-tempered face and kind eyes, and she thought she should like him.

"Bit tired, I expect?"

"Yes, thank you, I am," said Jessie shyly.

"Hullo, missis, been having a spring clean?" he asked comically, as he glanced about him. "The place looks so tidy I hardly knew it."

Mrs. Lang looked half annoyed. "New brooms sweep clean," she said shortly, "and two pairs of hands can do what one can't."

"That's true," said the young man soothingly. "I don't know how you ever managed to get through it all by yourself."

Mrs. Lang looked mollified. "It would have been all right if Harry would have lent a hand now and then," she said, "but he won't even clean his own boots, let alone any one else's; while as for bringing in a scuttle of coal, or going an errand, or putting a spade near the garden, he'd think himself disgraced for ever if he did either. Disgraced! He!" with a bitter laugh, and the meaning in her voice should have made her self-satisfied husband feel very small—if anything could have that effect on him.

Just at that moment heavy footsteps were heard approaching and conversation ceased.

"Here's your father coming," said Mrs. Lang in a lowered tone to Jessie. Then, as she stooped down to the oven to get out the dish of bacon for him, "We won't have ours now," she whispered to Jessie; "you and me'll have ours after they're gone, when there's a little peace and quietness," and Jessie, in spite of her hunger, which was making her feel quite sick and faint, felt glad.

"While you are waiting will you run up and talk to Charlie?" she asked kindly, for she saw Jessie's dread of her father, which was only too plainly written on her face.

"Who is Charlie?" Jessie asked, "and where is he? I'd like to go."

"You go up-stairs, and on the second landing from this you'll see four doors, one of the back ones is our bedroom, and the next one is Charlie's. He is my son, you know, he's just about your age, but he's—he's very delicate." Mrs. Lang hesitated a little, and turned her face away from Jessie for a moment. "He's got to lie in bed all the time, it is very dull for him, and he'll be glad to see you, he knows you are come."

The door was banged open and banged shut again. "What's the use of my taking the trouble to get up, in such weather as this, and shave myself, and—and put myself out like this," grumbled the master of the house, entering half dressed, half asleep, and more than half angry. "No horses can run—"

Jessie crept to the door and escaped as swiftly and silently as possible. At the sight of her father all her old terror of him rushed over her again, and she felt she could not face him.

Up the stairs she hurried as fast as the darkness and her own ignorance of the house would let her, then stopped suddenly. She did not know how many landings she had passed, or where to go. She tried to remember, but it was no good. "I'll go on a little further, though," she thought, "it will be better than going back again," and she groped her way carefully up another little flight of stairs. Round the bend of them a light gleamed from a partly open door. She went on further and looked in. The room was empty and very untidy, but there was a light burning in it. It was the one her father had just left. In the dimness she made out a smaller door beside it. Was this Charlie's? She listened for a moment, then a small thin voice called out, "Is anybody there? Who is it? Mother, is that you?"

Jessie stepped over to the door and knocked. "It is me—Jessie," she called back. "Your mother sent me up to see you. May I come in?"

"Yes, please."

Jessie turned the handle very carefully. She felt painfully shy now that she was actually here, but it was too late to turn back, so she sidled in around the door, wondering very much what she should see, and what she should say.

What she saw was an untidy room with a small bed in it, and a large window just opposite the bed. There were a few fairly good pieces of furniture in it as well, but the whole place looked neglected, untidy and comfortless. Jessie did not notice this so much just at first, though, for the little figure in the bed claimed most of her attention.

Charlie was really of the same age as herself, but he was so thin and worn and helpless, he looked much younger, and his pale little face wore something of the appealing look of a baby.

A great, great pity for him swelled up in Jessie's heart, and drove out most of her shyness. "I am *so* sorry you are ill," she said sympathetically. "Are you always like it?"

"Yes," said Charlie, looking at her with very shy, but very great interest. "I have been for a long time. I think it is seven years now. I fell backwards off a 'bus and hurt my back."

"Oh, what a dreadful thing!" exclaimed Jessie. "Couldn't a doctor cure you?"

"No. I was in hospital for nearly a year, but mother wanted me; she didn't like my being there, and when they said they couldn't make me well, mother said she would have me come home with her. She wanted me."

"Were you glad?"

"Yes. I was very glad. I wanted mother."

A short pause following, Jessie thought she had better introduce herself. "I am Jessie Lang," she said; "and—and I am come to live here, father says I must. I s'pose for always—to help your mother with the lodgers."

"Are you? How nice! I am so glad," cried Charlie; "then you'll be able to come and talk to me sometimes."

"I am not glad," said Jessie, with a quaver in her voice; "but I should like to come and talk to you as often as I can." Then presently she added, in a conflicting tone, "I don't know what to call your mother. I don't like to say 'Mrs. Lang,' it seems so— so silly and—stuck-up, and I don't like to call her 'mother,' because, you see, she isn't mine at all, really."

"I should," said Charlie decidedly. "I have to call your father 'father,' though I hate to. I don't like him. I hate him—he's— he's unkind to mother!" and the pale face flushed and the sad eyes filled with the strength of other feeling.

"Oh!" exclaimed Jessie, "you ought not to speak like that, I am sure. Why do you ha—why don't you like him?"

"'Cause he's so unkind to mother. He is unkind to me, too, but I don't mind that, I don't see him often; but he's always going on at mother, he makes her miserable, and he—he hits her!" staring at Jessie with wide, horrified eyes. "We were so happy and comfortable before he came, but now everything seems all wrong, and mother is always unhappy, and—and I—I can't bear it."

"Don't cry," said Jessie soothingly. "Did you live here always?"

"Yes, and we had nice lodgers, and a nice house, and we had money enough for what we wanted, but father costs such a lot, and takes nearly all the money mother gets, and he won't give her any of it. He won't work himself, either. All the nice lodgers left because he made such rows in the house, and was always quarrelling; there's only one of them left, that's Miss Patch. She has the attic right at the top of the house. She went up there because it is quieter."

He talked on eagerly in his old-fashioned way, his face flushing with weakness and excitement. It was such a rare treat to him to have any one to talk to, particularly any one of his own age—a sympathetic listener, too.

"Do you know Miss Patch yet?"

"No," said Jessie. "I only came last night very late. I've seen one lodger, a young man. He came down in the kitchen to his breakfast."

"Oh, Tom Salter! You'll like him—I do. I want my breakfast, don't you?"

"Yes," said Jessie, with a deep sigh. "I am *very* hungry, but— but—your mother said we would wait till father was gone." She hesitated over the term by which she should speak of her stepmother. Charlie noticed it.

"I wish you'd call her 'mother,'" he said gently; "it would make us seem more like brother and sister, and I would love to have a sister. I've wished so often that I'd got one, or had got somebody to talk to, and read and play with me. Mother would like it, too. She isn't really cross, you know. She is only tired and worried. You see, she's got me to look after, and me and father to keep, and ever so many lodgers. I am so glad you're come to help her. I do long to be able to, and I can only give her extra trouble." He spoke with sad earnestness far beyond his age.

A ray of comfort entered Jessie's sad heart. She felt really drawn towards her new stepbrother, and she loved to feel she was being useful.

"Yes, I'll help her," she said as brightly as she could for the weariness which was creeping over her. "I have been, a little, already. Can I help you? I'd love to try and make your room a little bit tidier."

"Does it look untidy?" asked Charlie, feeling somewhat taken aback.

It looked more than untidy, but Jessie was too polite to say so, and as she leaned against the bed she was planning in her mind what she could do to make it nicer for him.

"I wish I could get you some flowers," she said eagerly, "some out of our garden. Oh, we had such lots there, such lovely ones, roses, and violets, jessamine and lilac, and may—oh, all sorts. I had a garden of my own, too. Oh, I'd love to take you to granny's, and let you see it all!"

Charlie was watching her and listening with intense interest. "How sorry you must be to leave it all!" he remarked sympathetically. "I'd love to lie in a garden with flowers, and the bees humming, and no noise of rattling carts and milk-cans. Oh, Jessie!" but to his dismay Jessie buried her face in her hands and burst into tears.

"I can't stay here," she cried, "I can't, I can't! I *must* go home. I shall die if I don't go home to granp," and she sobbed and sobbed until Charlie was quite frightened.

"Jessie, don't—don't—don't cry like that. I'll ask mother to let you go, if you want to so badly—but I wish you didn't," he sighed, his own lips quivering. "I wish you would stay here. I want you *so* much, I am so lonely and dull, and—and I hoped you were come to stay."

Jessie's own tears were checked more quickly by the sight of his than they would have been by any other means. She pulled herself together as well as she could. "No—o, don't ask mother," she said in a choked, thick voice, "it is no use, father would make me stay, and it would only make him angry if we asked him, and I—I want to help you, too," she added, quite truthfully. "I shan't mind so much by and by, p'raps. Don't cry, Charlie.

Turn round and listen, and I'll tell you more stories. Then, after breakfast, I'll tidy your room."

The violence of Charlie's sobs had quite frightened away and stopped hers, and banished for a time her home-sickness. She put all her thoughts into her coaxing of Charlie, and after a time he raised his head and turned around and faced her, and while he lay back on his pillows, very weary after his excitement, Jessie, the more weary of the two, tried bravely to be cheerful, and to talk brightly, and so Mrs. Lang found them when, a little later, she brought up Charlie's breakfast on a tray.

Mrs. Lang even smiled when she saw the two together, evidently on such good terms, and the happy smile with which Charlie looked up at her delighted her sad heart. He was the apple of her eye, the great love of her life, the only thing in the world she cared for, and to see him happy, to see his dull, cheerless days brightened, gave her more pleasure than anything. She kissed her boy and looked quite kindly at Jessie.

"Your breakfast is ready in the oven," she said, "and I'm sure you must be famished. I am. I thought I should never get the men started off. Now, darling," to Charlie, "will you take your breakfast?" She put down the tray and raised him on his pillow a little. Jessie, accustomed now to invalids, beat up the pillow and placed it behind him.

"Is that right?" she asked.

"Oh yes, that's lovely," said Charlie, with a sigh of pleasure.

Mrs. Lang brought forward the tray. Jessie's eye fell on it with dismay. Trained by Miss Barley in dainty neatness, and by her grandmother in cleanness and care and thoughtfulness, the sight of it shocked her. The black dingy tray was smeared and dirty, the slice of bread rested on it, with no plate between, the knife and fork and cup were dirty too, and all was put down anyhow. Charlie probably was not accustomed to daintiness, but this was enough to check whatever appetite an invalid might have. Jessie longed to take the tray away, and set it according to her own notions, but she said nothing, for instinct told her that her mother's feelings would be hurt if she did, and that it would not be nice for a stranger to come in and begin to alter things according to her own tastes. She made up her mind, though, to try in small ways to make things nicer for the invalid when she got the opportunity.

CHAPTER IX
MISS PATCH

The opportunity Jessie yearned for came before long. One morning her mother had, unexpectedly, to go out very soon after breakfast.

"Jessie," she said, "I haven't been able to touch Charlie's room, more than to make his bed; you must tidy it while I am out. I shan't be very long, and there won't be anything more to do than just keep in the fire in the kitchen."

Jessie was delighted. As soon as her mother had gone she mounted to Charlie's room laden with brush and dustpan, and a bit of rag for a duster. Charlie looked up in astonishment when she came in, then with delight; he loved to have Jessie doing things for him, she did them so thoroughly and daintily.

"I am going to brush down the cobwebs first," said Jessie, "at least all that I can reach," she added thoughtfully, "so put your head right down under the clothes. I wish I had a dust-sheet, but it can't be helped, I must do without one. Now, steady! I am going to move your bed out from the wall. One, two, three, and be off!" and with a tug of her strong young arms she truckled the bed out into the middle of the room. Charlie was enraptured. He found it impossible to keep his head covered, dust or no dust.

"How funny it looks, and how nice, everything seems different. Jessie, don't you think my bed could stay out here?"

"Well, no," said Jessie, "it would be too much in the way stuck right out in the middle of the room, but I dare say mother wouldn't mind your having it somewhere else for a change. We'll try it, and ask her when she comes in," and Jessie quickly swept a clear space and pushed the bed back against the wall.

"Oh, that is nice!" said Charlie. "If I lie on my side a little I can look out of the window and see the houses opposite, and I haven't got the light shining right in on my eyes as I had before. It was dreadful when my head was aching."

"I thought it must be," said Jessie sympathetically, busily sweeping all the time. There was a great deal to be done, and she was very anxious to have it all looking nice by the time Mrs. Lang returned. She ran down with the bits of carpet and beat them, then she dusted the mantelpiece and the furniture, and arranged everything in the room to what, she thought, was the best advantage. She cleaned the window, too, which was a great improvement to the look of the room.

> Charlie was delighted. "Oh, it is nice! It looks like a new room, I feel as if I had gone away for a change. Everything seems different. Jessie, do go and ask Miss Patch to come and see it, will you? She'd love to."

Jessie flew away, willingly enough, and up the stairs until she came to the big attic at the very top of the house, which she knew was Miss Patch's. She had not spoken to Miss Patch yet, but she had heard a good deal about her from Charlie, who seemed very fond indeed of her, and often bemoaned the fact that she lived at the very top of the house now, for he very seldom saw her; she was lame and suffered a good deal, and could not get up and down the steep stairs very well, and he could not go up to her.

As she approached the door Jessie heard a sound of a soft voice singing, and paused a moment to listen, she could not bear to interrupt.

> "I may not tell the reason,
> 'Tis enough for thee to know
> That I, the Master, am teaching,
> And give this cup of woe."

The singing ceased for a moment, and Jessie gently knocked at the door.

"Come in," said the same voice brightly; "open the door, please, and come in."

Jessie did as she was bid, and stepped into one of the neatest and cleanest and oddest rooms she had ever seen in her life. The furniture in it was scanty, but what there was was old-fashioned and good, there was a bright rug on the floor, a few pictures on the walls at each end, an old-fashioned wooden bed at one side, a dear little round table before the fire, and a large arm-chair. The room was a large attic which really stretched over the whole of the top of the house, but though it was so large, there was really not very much available space in it, for the sides sloped steeply. Miss Patch had curtained off the sides, and out of the long narrow strip down the middle had formed, in Jessie's opinion, one of the nicest rooms she had ever seen.

The owner of the room looked up at Jessie with a bright smile, a smile which brightened still more when Jessie gave her message.

"Please, Charlie wants to know if you will come down and see his room. I have been tidying it a little, and I moved the bed, and he is so delighted with it he wants you to see it."

"I should like to, very much," said Miss Patch, "but I have rheumatism in my knee to-day, and I can't get up and down stairs very well. Perhaps, though," she added, with sudden thought, "you will help me?"

"Oh yes," said Jessie, advancing further into the room, "I would like to if I can. What shall I do?"

"I will ask you to let me lean on your shoulder a little, that is all, dear. But will you wait just a moment while I finish preparing the potatoes for my dinner?"

"Oh yes. I will wait, and—and—I'd like to help you," said Jessie, half eager, half shy. "Thank you, dear, but I've nearly done, and it isn't worth while for you to wet your hands. Sit down instead and talk to me. I heard that Mrs. Lang was having a little daughter to help her, and I have been hoping I should see you—but I haven't even heard your name yet!"

"It is Jessie."

"Oh, is it. I am very glad, for I had a dear little pupil once called by that name, and I have been fond of it ever since. She was really, though, christened 'Jessica.'"

"I am only *called* Jessie. I was christened Jessamine May," explained Jessie seriously. "Grandfather has got a jessamine growing all over the front of his house, and he has ever such beautiful red may-trees in the garden. They were there when mother was a little girl, and she loved them so dearly she called me after them, to keep her in mind of home."

"What a pretty name," said Miss Patch gently, "and what a beautiful thought. You are a little bit of a sweet garden transplanted into the midst of a dingy street to brighten us up, and bring beautiful and fragrant things to our minds. Jessamine and may blossom," she repeated softly; "oh, the picture it calls up, and the sweet fragrance! I seem to see them and to smell them, even here! I am ready now, little Jessamine May; shall we go to Charlie?"

Jessie sprang to her feet. "I think yours is such a pretty room," she said half timidly; and then her eye falling on a rose-bush in Miss Patch's window, all her timidity vanished, and she sprang towards it with a cry of mingled pleasure and pain.

"Oh, you have a rose-bush, too!" she cried eagerly. "I had one at granp's, and I loved it so." The quivering of her lips prevented her saying more, and the tears in her eyes made the rose-bush look all misty and dim.

Miss Patch saw and understood, and it was a very loving hand she laid on Jessie's shoulder. "I know, dear, I know how it feels—and you cannot understand the why and the wherefore of it all now—but you will some day—and in the meantime you are come to be a bit of sweet garden in our midst, to cheer us as your rose cheered you—and we do need some brightness here, little Jessamine May, I can assure you." And, somehow, Jessie felt much of her overwhelming sorrow vanish at the little old lady's words, and as she helped her down the stairs she felt quite cheered and happy again.

Charlie's delight more than repaid Miss Patch for the pain and effort of going down to see him, and whilst they were all looking and admiring, and agreeing what a wonderful improvement it was, and how much more comfortable and spacious the room looked, and in every way desirable, Mrs. Lang returned and came up-stairs to see how her boy had got on in her absence.

Jessie had been rather dreading this moment, for she could not help feeling that she had been taking a great liberty, but Mrs. Lang was too weary and anxious to make troubles of trifles, and anything that pleased her darling was sure to please her too.

So she expressed her approval of their doings and sat down on the foot of Charlie's bed to hear all about it, and all the advantages, and new charms and interests of having his bed in this position.

Miss Patch sat on the rickety chair and joined in occasionally, but her quick sympathy was aroused by the weariness on Mrs. Lang's face.

"You look tired out," she said kindly.

"I feel so," said Mrs. Lang listlessly. "The wind is almost more than any one can battle with, and the damp seems to get into one's bones. I feel ready to drop—and, oh, I've such a lot to do!"

"Mother," said Jessie eagerly, "shall I make you a cup of tea? I know the kettle is boiling by this time. Don't you think it would do you good?"

Charlie's face lit up again. "Oh do, mother, do, and have it up here, and Miss Patch have one, too, and Jessie, and me."

"Well, I declare!" cried Mrs. Lang, quite taken aback. "What next! I never heard of such a thing! I believe, though, that one would do me good, and I know I'd enjoy it ever so much. Miss Patch would, too, I believe!"

Miss Patch smiled. "I'd enjoy one," she laughed, "if I had to get up in the middle of the night for it."

Without waiting for another word Jessie flew off to the kitchen. This was her chance she felt to do things nicely, so, while the kettle came to the boil, she polished the shabby tray and the tea-cups and spoons. She had no pretty white cloth to lay on the tray, unfortunately, but she had a sheet of white paper that she had saved from a parcel, and she spread this on the tray, then arranged on it the cups and saucers and milk-jug and sugar-basin. She made the tea next and put out some biscuits on a plate.

She could not carry all up at once, so she took the tray first, then came back for the teapot and kettle. A second chair was got from Mrs. Lang's bedroom, and then the sociable little meal was begun.

It did not last long, but half-an-hour, at the longest. Yet it was one of those bright little spots which linger long in the memory and make one glad, though sometimes sad, to look back upon.

"Well, I must get on, my work won't do itself, I guess," sighed Mrs. Lang, at last reluctantly preparing to rise, but Charlie put out his hand to detain her.

"Don't go yet, mother, wait a minute, I want Miss Patch to
sing. Miss Patch, you will sing to us, just once, won't you?"
he pleaded. "That one you used to sing to me. Oh, do!
please! please!"

"But, my dear, my dinner is on cooking, and—and"—Miss Patch's cheeks flushed a delicate pink, she was very shy—"I—I ain't accustomed to singing, except to myself, and—well, I used to sing to you sometimes when you were very little and didn't know what good singing was."

"It was lovely," said Charlie earnestly, "and nobody ever sings to me now," he added wistfully.

Miss Patch's tender heart was touched, and her shyness overcome. "Very well, dear, I will," she agreed bravely, and it was really brave of her, for to do so cost her a great effort. "Perhaps we could choose a hymn we all know, and we could all join in. I am sure we all know 'Safe in the arms of Jesus,' or 'There's a home for little children.' You know them, don't you, Jessamine May?"

"Yes," said Jessie, "granp and I used to sing them on Sunday afternoons."

But when they had begun "There's a home for little children," Miss Patch was soon left to sing it through alone, for Charlie was too exhausted, and after the first line or so Mrs. Lang could not get out another word for the pain at her heart and the lump in her throat, and taking Charlie in her arms she sat with bowed head looking down at him.

"Would it be better—for him," she thought heart-brokenly, "would not that home be better than this—the only one she could give him—and what was to become of him if he lost her?" But she forced the thought away. "And what is to become of me—if I lose him?" she asked herself fiercely—and found no answer.

The last verse was reached, and she felt almost glad, the pain and the pathos were more than she could bear.

"Now, one more," pleaded Charlie's weak voice from the shelter of his mother's arms, and Miss Patch in her thin, sweet voice sang to a plaintive chanting air of her own the beautiful hymn written by Miss M. Betham-Edwards—

> "God make my life a little light
>   Within the world to glow;
> A little flame that burneth bright
>   Wherever I may go."
>
> "God made my life a little flower,
>   That giveth joy to all,
> Content to bloom in native bower
>   Although its place be small."
>
> "God make my life a little staff,
>   Whereon the weak may rest,
> That so what health and strength I have
>   May serve my neighbours best."

"It isn't a real tune," she explained shyly, when she had reached the end. "I liked the words so much that I learnt them by heart, and they ran in my head until I found myself singing them to any sort of drone that would fit them."

"I think it is all lovely," said Charlie; "don't you, Jessie?"

"Oh, *lovely*," breathed Jessie softly. She was too deeply impressed to be able to talk much. "God make my life a little flower," the words repeated themselves again in her brain. "Miss Patch called me a piece of sweet garden. I wonder—" But what Jessie wondered she could not put into words.

In a vague way, that she scarcely as yet understood, it had suddenly come home to her that, perhaps, after all it was for some good purpose that she had been called upon to bear all that she had to bear. Without those sweet, happy years at Springbrook she could never have come as a little piece of sweet garden to this sad corner of the world. Perhaps God had something for her—even a little girl like herself—to do for Him. And she would try her utmost, she determined—yes, her utmost; to do her best in the new life she had been called to, and to make others happier by her presence.

CHAPTER X
CHARLIE REACHES HOME

After that exciting morning, Jessie saw Miss Patch always once a day, at least, for she never failed to go up to her room to ask her if she could do any errands, or anything else for her, and very, very glad Miss Patch was, many a time, to be saved the long drag down all the stairs and up again, and the walk through the cold wet streets during the bitter winter months.

Being saved this much exertion, she was able to get down oftener to see Charlie, and both he and Jessie loved these visits of hers. More than once, too, when her husband was away, Mrs. Lang came for a brief spell, and they had tea together again in Charlie's room.

It was on one of the occasions when she was alone with Miss Patch that Jessie told of her Sunday-school in the garden, or by the fireside, with her grandfather. Her tears fell as she told of it, and her deep grief broke out uncontrollably, but Miss Patch did not try to check her story, she let her tell it all, thinking it would be better for her.

"And I've never been to Sunday-school, or to church since," she sobbed. "Father won't let me."

It was to Miss Patch, too, that she sobbed out the story of that dreadful day, and her grief for her grandparents and their suspense. "It would not be so bad," she moaned, "if father would Let me write to them and tell them I am well and—and safe, and—and not so very unhappy; and I wouldn't mind so much if I knew how they were, but granny was ill, and I know granp would feel it dreadfully losing me like that and never knowing what had become of me. They don't know where I am, or if I am alive or dead, and—and it has nearly killed them, I expect!" and her tears choked her.

"Will not your father let you write?" asked Miss Patch in a husky voice. The cruelty of it all made her kind heart ache with pain and indignation.

Jessie shook her pretty head mournfully. "No. He says it would unsettle me, and they would be always worrying round, and he wants peace and quietness—but, oh, Miss Patch, they loved me so, it must have nearly broken their hearts! And—and I love them so, I feel sometimes I can't bear it, I can't, I can't. I feel I *must* run away and find my way back to them. I am sure "—hopefully—" I could."

Miss Patch laid her thin hand very kindly on Jessie's bowed head. "Don't ever do that, dear! Don't ever set yourself against God's will. You are told in the Bible to obey your God and your earthly father, and God must have sent you here for some good purpose, dear. Perhaps to teach you something we cannot understand yet, perhaps to bring help and happiness to—to others, to your mother, and dear little Charlie there, and—and me.

> "God make my life a little staff,
>   Whereon the weak may rest,
>   That so what health and strength I have
>   May serve my neighbours best.

"I think that is what God wants you for, little flower, to help us and bring joy to us in this gloomy corner of the world; and, oh, my dear, you have such chances here. And if you go on trusting and hoping, little Jessamine, trying to hold the faith that never faileth, all will come right. I know it will, I am sure."

Jessie lifted a very eager face to her old friend. "Do you really think so?" she asked anxiously.

"I am sure of it, dear; quite sure."

Silence fell on them both for a few moments, then Jessie looked up with a face alight with eagerness. "Miss Patch, couldn't I have a little Sunday-school for Charlie, just like granp had for me? I couldn't teach him, but I could read to him, and learn hymns with him, couldn't I? Don't you think it would be nice?"

"I think it is a beautiful idea," agreed Miss Patch warmly. Then, after a moment, she added, "How would you like it if I had the school, and you both came to me? I could go down to Charlie's room, as a rule, but I do believe that sometimes you might both come up to me. If he were carried up very carefully and laid on my bed I feel sure it would not hurt him, and I think the change of surroundings might even do him good. What do you think of that plan?" and Miss Patch looked nearly as eager as Jessie by the time she had finished speaking.

Jessie had sprung to her feet with excitement. "I think it is perfectly lovely," she cried, "perfectly lovely! Shall we begin next Sunday? Oh, do, please! and may I go down and tell Charlie? He will be *so* glad. Thank you ever and ever so much," and putting up her hands she drew Miss Patch's thin face down to her own and kissed it warmly.

Charlie was as delighted as Jessie, and the prospect of going up to Miss Patch's room for an hour or so filled him with joyful excitement. Mrs. Lang was pleased, too. Anything that gave Charlie pleasure was sure to give her pleasure, and she was thankful for any means of teaching him and giving him new interests.

No one told Harry Lang about it, for he took no interest in anything they did, and they knew too well that his crooked temper would find delight in putting a stop to any little scheme they made. Tom Salter knew, though, for having met Mrs. Lang one day struggling up the stairs with Charlie in her arms, wrapped in blankets, he insisted on carrying him up for her, every time he went, after that, and when he was asked to stay, he did stay, and listened to Miss Patch reading, and joined in the hymns, and after the first time he came quite often.

Jessie was delighted, she liked Tom Salter, for though he spoke but little, he had often done her a kindness, helping her carry a heavy scuttle of coal up the stairs, or a pail of water; and many a time, of a Saturday night, he cleaned several pairs of the lodgers' boots for her in readiness for Sunday; and many other kindly acts he had done, that meant much to the little over-burthened worker, for Jessie's life was a hard one in those days.

Miss Patch took care of her own room, and required no attention, but there were two lodgers in the front rooms on each landing, and all required meals cooked and carried to their rooms mornings and evenings, their rooms swept and dusted, their boots cleaned, and a hundred little attentions, and to Jessie it seemed as though she spent most of her life on the stairs, on her way up or down, generally carrying heavy trays or a load of some sort.

Then there were the beds to help to make, windows to clean, rooms and stairs to sweep, and numberless other duties. Fortunately, Jessie liked housework, and Mrs. Dawson might well have been proud of her pupil, could she have seen the difference that by degrees crept over the look of the house, both inside and out, as time went on.

The windows were kept bright now, and the sills whitened; the doorsteps, which used to be so dirty and neglected, were now kept swept and whitened, too; and the lodgers appreciated the change, and said so more than once.

So the days and weeks passed by, and the weeks became months, and soon the months had become a whole year. Jessie could not believe it when Charlie first drew her attention to the fact. A whole year!

What could have become of poor granny and granp all this time! She wondered if they ever wept and wept, and longed for her as she did for them. Sometimes, when the wind howled, or some one played sad music in the streets, she felt as though her heart would break with its weight of sad longing.

Fortunately for her, her days were too full and busy to allow of constant repining; and at night she was too weary to lie awake long grieving. Miss Patch had said, "Have faith and trust and all will come right some day," and Jessie did try to have faith, and to trust hopefully, though she worked hard and the fond poor, though her father was neglectful and cruel, and her mother gloomy and reserved.

> "God make my life a little flower,
>   That giveth joy to all,
>   Content to bloom in native bower,
>   Although its place be small."

She sang, and she did try hard to be content, and to do what she could, and the result was that in many ways she was happy in spite of all.

She loved Miss Patch, and the lonely little old woman loved her, and helped her over many a stony bit of road. Charlie loved her, and clung to her, too, and her mother, she fancied, was fond of her in her own quiet, cold way. At any rate, she never beat her, as her father did, or scolded and bullied her. But soon after her second year in London had begun a new trouble, and a very heavy one, came to Jessie. Charlie, she was sure, was getting worse.

He was growing thinner, and paler, and feebler, week by week. The first time the truth dawned on her was one Sunday, when he said languidly that he thought he would not go up to Miss Patch's room that afternoon, he was too tired.

Jessie was so astounded that for a second or so she could only stand and stare at him. Then, with a sudden sharp fear at her heart, she flew to his side.

"Aren't you feeling very well?" she asked anxiously, and Charlie shook his head, but with tears in his eyes, tears of weakness and disappointment.

"Shall I ask Miss Patch to come down here?" she asked presently, longing to rouse and cheer him. But he only shook his head again.

"No, thank you, it would be too much trouble for her, and—don't you think it would be nice to stay quiet, just by ourselves, this afternoon?" he asked. "Will you read to me, or tell me about Springbrook?"

"Of course I will, dear," she answered warmly; "but—but I had better go up and tell Miss Patch, hadn't I, or she would think it unkind?"

This, though, was not her only reason for going. She wanted to be alone, away from him for a moment, to try and recover herself, and face this new shock.

"Miss Patch," she cried in a tone of agony, "I believe Charlie is worse, he seems so quiet, and so tired, and—and—Oh, Miss Patch, what shall I do! He *must* get better, he must, he must."

But the tears came into Miss Patch's eyes too, and she had little comfort to offer. She had long had grave fears, and though she had tried to put them aside, she had never quite succeeded.

But Jessie had to control herself, for Charlie was waiting for her. "When these fogs are gone, and the spring comes, and the sunshine," she said, trying to pluck up hope, "he will be better, I am sure."

"This weather certainly tries the strongest," said Miss Patch, with a sigh. "We will hope for the best, dear. We all of us have our bad days, don't we? Charlie may be much better to-morrow; we must try to keep his spirits up, and make him as cheerful and happy as we can." But Jessie, as she went down the stairs again, wondered how that would be possible when she herself felt so far from being either.

Christmas came and went, and the spring came, but without bringing to Charlie the strength and health that Jessie prayed for so earnestly for him. He never again went up to Miss Patch's room to Sunday-school, so Miss Patch came down to him, and read or sang to him, just as he wished. They had no lessons now, for he could not bear even that slight strain, and, as Miss Patch said, with tears trickling down her worn cheeks—

"What good is my teaching now? He will soon know more than any of us. We can only help and strengthen him for the last hard steps of his journey." And Tom Salter, to whom she spoke, said huskily—

"You'd be a help to anybody, miss; don't 'ee give way now, don't 'ee give way," and all the time he was wiping the back of his hand across his own wet eyes. "'Tisn't *his* journey that'll be the hardest and stormiest, I'm thinking," added Tom, "'tis those he'll leave behind. Who is going to break it to his mother? She doesn't seem to see it for herself—though how she can help it is past my understanding."

Poor Miss Patch's hands shook, and her tears fell faster. "I can't, I can't," she murmured, "but yet—I suppose I ought—there's nobody else to do it."

It was Charlie himself, though, who saved her that pain. "Mother," he said one evening, when she came to get him ready for the night, "would you be very unhappy if I went away from you?"

"What do you mean?" she cried, in sudden fear. "You—you—"

"Would you, mother?" he persisted.

"Be unhappy! Why, I should break my heart—you are all I have to care for, or live for, or—"

He put his little wasted arm about her neck, and drew her frightened face down to his. "Mother, when I go away you will know I am happy—but Jessie has gone away from her poor old granp and granny, and they don't know—they think she is very unhappy and badly treated, and— and, mother, I want you to try and get father to let Jessie go back to them again, they must be so dreadfully sad about her. I often think about them—I can't help it—and it makes me feel so sad." He was silent for a moment. "I wish I could see them," he added dreamily, "that I could tell them how I love her, and how kind she has been to me, and—and that she isn't so *very* unhappy."

Mrs. Lang had stood staring down at him speechless, stricken suddenly numb and dumb with an awful overwhelming terror.

"Charlie—you—you ain't feeling ill—worse—are you? What's the matter, dear? Why do you talk so? What do you mean by 'when you go away'?" Her lips could scarcely form the last words, for she knew as well as he could tell her. It had come suddenly to her understanding that he was going a long, long journey—and soon; the last journey, from which there was no returning.

With a heart-broken cry she fell on her knees by the bed. "You ain't going, you shan't! Charlie, you shan't go away from me—you must stay with me till I go too—"

"You will come to me, mother, but I shall go first, and I'll tell God all about how you have had to work, and how hard it has been for you, and He will understand—"

"You can't—you mustn't go! Oh, my dear, my dear, don't leave me."

"Oh, mother, I am *so* tired, and I—I think I want to go, but I want you to come too. You will, won't you, mother?" and he tried again to draw her face down to his.

"I will try," she promised faintly, and then burst into a passion of heart-broken sobs.

A month later, when in the country the hedges were full of primroses and violets, and pure little daisies, Charlie took the last steps of his painful journey, and reached the "rest" for which he craved.

It was on a Saturday that his brief journey through this life ended, and on the Sunday those whom he had loved—his mother, and Jessie, Miss Patch and Tom Salter—gathered in the little bare, quiet bedroom, with him in the midst of them once more, but so silent now, so very quiet and still.

"I am sure he is with us in spirit, the darling," said Miss Patch softly, as she looked at the worn little face, so peaceful now, and free from the drawn lines of pain they had worn hitherto; and, while they all knelt around his bed, she said a few simple prayers, such as went straight to their sad hearts, and sowed the germs, at least, of comfort there; and while they still knelt, thinking their own sad thoughts, her sweet voice broke softly into song.

> "Sleep on, beloved, sleep and take thy rest.
> Lay down thy head upon thy Saviour's breast,
> We love thee well, but Jesus loves thee best—
> Good-night!"

The others knelt, rapt, breathless, afraid to move lest they should break the spell and the sweet singing, or lose one of the beautiful words. Through the whole exquisite hymn she continued until the last verse was reached—

> "Until we meet again before His throne,
> Clothed in the spotless robes He gives His own,
> Until we know, even as we are known;—
> Good-night!"

Voice and words died away together. Then one by one they rose and, bending over him, kissed him fondly.

"Good-night, little Charlie, 'good-night,' not 'good-bye.'"

CHAPTER XI
TOO LATE

When Harry Lang was told that Charlie was dead, he looked shocked for the moment, then, having remarked glibly that "it was all for the best," and "at any rate he wouldn't suffer any more," he told Jessie to make haste and get him some food, and became absorbed in making his own plans for his own comfort.

He hated trouble, and sadness, and discomfort of others' making, and he made up his mind at once to go away out of it for a time, and not return until the funeral, at any rate, was over. So at the end of his meal he announced to Jessie that he had to go away for a week on business. He wouldn't bother her mother by telling her about it now, while she was worn out and trying to rest, but Jessie could tell her by and by.

What he should have done, of course, was to remain at home and relieve his poor stricken wife of all the painful details that necessarily followed the seeing about the little coffin, the grave, and the funeral. But Harry Lang had trained people well for his own purposes. No one ever expected assistance of any kind from him; so, instead of missing him, most people felt his absence as only a great relief. Mrs. Lang and Jessie did so now.

At the end of ten days he came back again, expecting to find not only the funeral a thing of the past, but all feelings of loss and sorrow to be put away out of sight and memory.

"You'll be able to take in another lodger now," he remarked abruptly to his wife as he ate his supper on the night of his return. "There's a friend of mine that'll be glad to take the room, and he'll have his breakfast and supper here with me, just as Tom Salter does."

Mrs. Lang did not speak until he had finished; then, without looking at him, she answered curtly, "I am not taking any more lodgers."

Her husband looked up in sudden rage and astonishment. He had never heard his wife speak like that before, and it gave him quite a shock.

"Not—not—" he gasped; "and whose house is this, I'd like to know; and who, may I ask, is master here?"

"The house belongs to the one that pays the rent. This house is mine, and I am master here, and mistress too," she answered coldly but firmly; "and if I did want another lodger, I shouldn't take a friend of yours; I am going to keep my house respectable, as far as I can—or give it up."

Harry Lang's voice completely failed him, and he sat silently staring at his wife in wide-eyed amazement. He had thought he had long ago killed all the spirit in her, and here she was declaring her independence in the calmest manner possible, and actually defying him—and he could find nothing to say or do! Her tone to him, and the opinion, it was only too evident, she held of him, hurt and mortified him more than he had ever thought possible; for in his own opinion he had always been a tremendously fine fellow, very superior indeed to those poor creatures who went tamely to work, day after day, and handed their money over to their wives; and he thought every one else was of the same opinion.

"I—I think trouble or something has turned your brain!" he stuttered at last, "and you had better look sharp and get it right again, I can tell you, or I'll know the reason why."

"My brain is all right," said Mary Lang quietly; "trouble has turned my heart, perhaps, and that isn't likely ever to get right again; but I don't see that that can matter to you. You never cared for me or my heart, or how I felt, or how anybody else felt, but yourself."

"I care about Bert Snow coming here to lodge, and he's coming, too! Do you hear? I told him he could, and I ain't going to be made to look small—"

"You won't look any smaller," said his wife reassuringly, and he wondered stupidly exactly what she meant, or if she meant anything. "You must tell your friend he cannot come here, I haven't got a room for him. I am not going to have such as he in Charlie's room. Jessie is to have it, and it's about time, I think, that your daughter had a bed and a room fit for her to sleep in," she added scathingly.

Harry Lang did not care in the least whether Jessie had or had not a bed, or if she slept on the doorstep; but he cared very much about his friend, and he meant to have his own way. But though he stormed, and bullied, and even struck his wife, he found her, for the first time, as firm as adamant, and quite as indifferent to him. His orders meant nothing to her, and the change in her impressed him very much.

So Jessie, for the first time since she left Springbrook, had a real bedroom again, and a place she could call her own. She did not quite like using it, but she felt that her mother wished it. Mrs. Lang would have liked to keep the little room always sacred to the memory of him who had spent most of his little life in it, but rather Jessie should have it than that it should be desecrated by a betting, drinking, gambling stranger, who would pollute it, she felt, by his presence!

So Jessie and her possessions were installed. It was not a long business, for her belongings were very few. She had not had a penny or a gift of any kind since she came to London, except a little book of hymns that Miss Patch had given her, and one of Charlie's favourite books which he had wished her to have. Her little stock of clothing had never been added to since she came, until now, when her stepmother seemed to find pleasure in providing her with a very thorough outfit of mourning.

Now that she had lost her boy, the one and only joy that was hers, Mrs. Lang seemed to turn to Jessie with more real affection than she had ever shown before. Jessie had loved her dead darling, and any one who had loved him or been good to him had all the grateful devotion of the poor mother's aching heart.

Charlie's little room was re-papered and painted, his little bed was put away, and another bought for Jessie, and on the floor was spread a new rug. Jessie soon grew to take quite a pride in her little room. She scrubbed the floor every week, and polished the window until it put to shame most of the windows in the neighbourhood. Miss Patch gave her a piece of pretty chintz to hang at the back of her looking-glass, and Tom Salter actually brought her home one day a china vase to stand on her mantelpiece. Jessie was proud and pleased sure enough then! and, as time went on, and she grew to miss Charlie less, she would have been quite happy if she might but have written to her grandfather and grandmother, or could have had some tidings of them.

But month after month went by, and still the same
suspense continued. She did not even know if they were
alive or dead.

Lodgers came and went, some pleasant, some very much the reverse; some kind, some exacting. Jessie worked early and late at school and at home. The school did not count for much in her life, and she made no real friends amongst the children. Her earlier delicate training made her feel she was not one of them; their speech and manners jarred on her, and having lived most of her life with grown-ups, she had no knowledge of games, or play, nor any skill in either, and their tastes did not interest her, nor hers interest them. She would far rather sit with Miss Patch, and talk or read to her, or be read to. Miss Patch was teaching her some different kinds of needlework, and while Jessie worked her teacher would read to her; and those readings in that peaceful room were Jessie's greatest delight.

Then one day, when they least expected it, came an end to it all, and all the ordinary everyday life they had lived together in that house for months past was finished by a violent knocking at the front door. At least that was the first sign they had of the change that was impending!

> Such a knocking it was! it echoed through the house, and
> up and down the street, making them both spring to their
> feet in dire alarm. Miss Patch gave a sharp cry and her
> hand flew to her side. Jessie's face blanched, and her eyes
> grew dark with fear.

"Who can it be!" she gasped; "who—what—what can have happened?" Mrs. Lang was out, gone to the cemetery, so there was no one to answer the knock but Jessie herself, and realizing it she ran trembling down the stairs. She had delayed only a moment, but before she reached the foot of the stairs there came another knock, longer and louder than the first. Jessie threw herself on the door and flung it open. A man was standing on the step, evidently trying to keep himself from making another assault on the door. He seemed almost beside himself with excitement or fright, or something very like both.

"Where's your mother?" he demanded impatiently.

"Out," said Jessie shortly, something in the man's manner increased her alarm until she could scarcely utter a word. "She's—gone—to the cemetery," she gasped in explanation. "I think—she'll be— home—soon."

The day was already waning, and the sun going down. She looked out anxiously, longing to see her mother come into sight. The man gave an impatient click of his tongue.

"What am I to do?" he demanded testily, gazing anxiously up and down the street, but as he seemed to be addressing only the air, or himself, Jessie did not feel obliged or able to make any suggestion.

"Look here," he said, turning quickly round to her, "there has been an accident, and—and I came to—to—break it to your mother. I know her and your—your father. I lived here once, and—and I thought it might be kind to break it to her before the police came for her."

Jessie's heart almost stood still with fright. "The p'lice," she gasped, "for mother!—oh, what has happened?"

"There's been an accident to your father; there was a bit of a fight in the train coming home from the races, and—and he got flung against the door, and it opened—and he fell out."

A low cry of horror broke from Jessie. Instinct told her that the news was very serious. If her father had not been severely injured— or worse, the man would not have been so upset.

"Is—is—" she gasped.

"He is taken to the hospital," responded the man quickly, almost as though he was anxious to check her next question.

"Ah! there is mother!" cried Jessie in a tone of infinite relief, as she saw her appear at the gate. Mrs. Lang looked very white and very tired, and an expression of vague fear came into her eyes as they fell on pale, trembling Jessie, and the stranger, also pale and evidently greatly agitated. She lived always in a state of dread of some disaster or disgrace, and instinct told her that one or the other had come.

The man went down the steps to meet her. Jessie stood waiting at the door; she would have gone forward too, but that she was shaking so, she felt she should never get down the steps. So she stood there supporting herself by the door, and watched her mother's face, and saw the shocked look that came over it. She could not hear all that was said, but she caught fragments of sentences, "Come at once"— "alive when I left." "Searching him for his name and address, but I knew Harry—and came along to prepare you. He's at St. Mary's."

Mrs. Lang came up to the door to Jessie, holding out her basket and umbrella for her to take. She dragged her limbs almost like a paralyzed woman, and her eyes looked dazed. "I'll be back—as soon as I can," she said; but her lips seemed stiff and scarcely able to move. "You look after the house." She was turning away, when she suddenly turned, and stooping, kissed Jessie for the first time in her life; and Jessie, looking up, flung her arms around her stepmother's neck and kissed her in return. This new trouble had brought them very close.

With tear-blinded eyes Jessie turned and groped her way back into the house to face that hardest of all trials—suspense. Slowly, slowly she dragged herself down to the kitchen to see to the fire, then up the stairs to Miss Patch to tell her the news and wait.

Before long, though, they both crept down to the kitchen, so as to be at hand when needed; but Jessie could not keep still, the suspense was hard to bear, and made her restless. She wandered aimlessly from fire to window and back again. They talked a little, speculating as to what was happening, and what they should hear, and Jessie lit the lamps as soon as the dimness gave her the slightest excuse. A great dread of troubles and changes, and they knew not what else, filled them both.

Fortunately the suspense did not last very long. Before two hours had passed they heard footsteps coming up the path to the house. Jessie knew them, and flew out to meet her mother. Miss Patch stirred the fire into a cheerful blaze, then smiled to herself at the uselessness of her own act. She longed to do so much, yet was able to do so little.

Mrs. Lang came in slowly, heavily; her face was white, her eyes were red.

"He is dead," she gasped, as she dropped heavily into a chair. "He is dead!" and her voice grew high and shrill and quavering.

"Poor soul, poor soul," sighed Miss Patch softly. "Did he suffer much? I hope he was spared that."

"He was never conscious, he—he—had no time to be sorry—to repent, or try to be better. He was struck down in the midst of all his wickedness and folly, with lying and cheating and bad language all about him. His last feeling was passion—and so he died—and I feel that I am as bad as any of them, I never tried to save him," and the poor widow laid her head on her outstretched arms and sobbed uncontrollably.

Miss Patch laid her thin arm around the shaking shoulder. "You did. My dear, you did. When first you knew him you were always trying."

"And then I got tired and gave up, and never tried any more, and we drifted further and further away—and now it is too late. He is dead, dead in all his sinfulness!"

Jessie crept away and up to her own little room. It was dark there and peaceful; the street outside was unusually quiet, awed into silence, for the time, by the tragedy in their midst—for the news had spread like wildfire.

The window was open, and up in the steely blue sky the moon was sailing, large, peaceful, grand. Jessie knelt by the window and gazed up at the sky and the moon, awed and wondering. She was dazed and overcome by all that had happened. Then she buried her face in her hands and prayed that her mother might be comforted.

She tried to think of some good deeds her father had done; but, alas, poor child, she could think of none, though it seemed treacherous to his memory to try, and fail.

Two days later Harry Lang was laid in his grave. Quite a crowd attended his funeral, but only four "mourners," and the chief of those four were the two he had wronged most, his widow and his child. Tom Salter, who had shown himself kind and helpful and full of thought in this terrible time, went to support the widow, and Miss Patch, in spite of her lameness, and pain, and weakness, went too, as a mark of respect to those that were left, and as a companion for poor Jessie.

Everything was done as nicely and carefully as though the dead man had been the best of husbands and fathers; no outward mark of respect was lacking; but, though none spoke it aloud, each one felt, as they returned to the empty house, that there was none of that awful sense of blankness, of loss, of heartrending silence, which usually fills the house that death has visited, the feeling that something is gone which can never, never return. There was, instead, almost a sense of relief, a feeling of peace. They all tried not to feel it, and nothing would have made them admit it, even to themselves; but it was there—one of the most sad and awe-inspiring feelings of that dreadful day.

Tom Salter left them as soon as he had seen them home, and went up to his room to change into his every-day clothes. His young, almost boyish face was very grave and thoughtful. "God help me never to live to leave such a feeling behind me," he thought to himself solemnly.

Life after this should have settled down into the usual groove again, and so Jessie thought, with the difference that a great discomfort and ever-present dread would be gone. Somehow, though, it did not.

Mrs. Lang, looking ill, and worn to a shadow, seemed grave and abstracted, and full of thoughts which she did not share with any one. She was often absent, too, on business of which she did not speak. At first Jessie noticed none of all this, she thought her mother's manner was simply the result of the shock and the trouble she had been through; then, by degrees, it came to her that things were different, that there was something in the air that she could not understand or explain, but she felt that changes were impending.

Often when she looked up she found her mother gazing at her wistfully, it seemed, and questioningly. More than once, too, she drew Jessie on to talk of her old home and her grandparents, and of her longing to see them again; and then one day her mother came to her and asked her if she remembered her grandfather's address!

Jessie knew then that her surmises were correct, and her heart beat fast with wonderment and hopes and fears, and a thousand questions poured through her brain.

CHAPTER XII
SPRINGBROOK AGAIN

Thomas Dawson was sitting in his chair in the garden enjoying the warmth of the October sunshine. The weather was unusually warm for the time of the year, and the little breeze which blew across the garden was very acceptable. The long graceful tendrils of the jessamine rose and fell like soft green waves above his head, a little cloud of dust rose and skidded along the road, to the annoyance of some lazy cows being driven home to the milking.

But Thomas heeded none of these things, he sat with his head sunk on his breast, his eyes staring gloomily before him, his thoughts far away. He had aged ten years and more in the last two. A very slight sound, though from within the house, roused him in an instant and brought him to his feet.

"I'm coming, mother, I'm coming," he called, and went indoors. "I expect it's pretty nigh tea-time, isn't it?" he asked, with affected cheerfulness; "the fire only wants a stir, and the kettle'll boil in no time."

Patience nodded and took up the poker. She was very slow of speech in those days, but it was a grand relief to know that she could speak at all, and break the silence which had held her for weeks and months after the stroke of paralysis which had seized her on that dreadful day when Harry Lang had stolen Jessie from them.

Thomas, coming back from market that night, had found his wife unconscious and helpless, and when at last she had recovered her senses it was long before she could speak and explain something of the terrible happenings of that afternoon; and even now, at the end of two years, her speech was still thick and slow, and her limbs on one side partially helpless.

Thomas spread the cloth on the table, and placed the china on it for her to arrange. The old man waited on his wife like a mother on her child, and nothing could exceed his patient devotion. With her he was always bright and cheery, and only his bowed back and snow-white hair and altogether aged appearance told of his own consuming grief and anxiety.

He cut the bread and butter, and made the tea with all the deftness of a woman. Patience watched him with the tears smarting behind her lids. When he had filled their cups he sat down, facing the window, and looking out along the garden to the little gate. They did not talk much. Thomas's mind had gone back to that morning when he had looked out and seen Daniel Magor at the gate with letters in his hand—that wonderful letter which had so altered and beautified their existence for a time, only to blight them both cruelly.

"I believe it's Miss Grace I see coming in," he said presently, rousing with a start. "She's at the gate, and—yes, she's unfastening it. I'll go and meet her."

On his way through the garden he saw a cat lazily basking on his best wall-flower seedlings, and drove her away; the excitement of it prevented his noticing the expression of Miss Grace's face, the anxious, excited look in her eyes.

"Good-evening, Mr. Dawson," she said, as she came close. "I was at the post office getting my letters, and there was one lying there for you, so I said I would bring it, as it was marked 'Urgent.' It seemed wrong to leave it there until to-morrow, I thought it might be important."

She handed him the envelope, but she did not turn and go. "I think I'll step in and speak to Mrs. Dawson for a moment or so," she said quietly, "just while you look at your letter, then I'll go, that you may talk it over with her."

She felt that her little scheme was rather a clumsy one, but she had a strong conviction that it might be well for her to be there just then. "I will go inside," and she left him standing there in the autumn sunlight staring at the letter he held in his trembling hands. He turned it over several times before he would make up his mind to open it. There was always a dread overshadowing him in those days of what he might have to hear.

Miss Grace had barely got through her first greetings, and declined Patience's offer of a cup of tea "fresh-made," when the door was flung open and Thomas almost fell in. In trouble he would have remembered his wife's affliction, and have hedged her round with every care, but joy was another thing. It was on joy that he had built his hopes of restoring her to her former self—and here it was, in his grasp!

"Mother!—Jessie!—I've heard from her!! Mother, mother, do you hear, there's news of her at last?"

Miss Grace stepped nearer and stood by the poor old woman, laying a firm hand on her shoulder, she could see how she was shaking. "If it is good news, tell her quickly," she said anxiously.

Thomas read the expression of Miss Grace's face, and recovered himself at once. His care for Patience was always his first thought.

"Good! My dear, yes, good as good can be. Better than I ever hoped for. She is well, and she's coming back, to *us*, mother! do you hear? She is coming back for good. It doesn't seem possible, it doesn't seem as though it can be true, yet it says so on the letter. Hark to it—in't it like the dear child herself speaking?"

The terrified look which had come into Patience's face died away. She could not speak, but she put out one shaking hand and thrust it into that of her husband, and so they read the glad news. It was a curious, excited, incoherent letter, but it told them all they wanted to know, for the time, at any rate.

"My Dearest Granp,

> "I have been longing to write all this time and tell you where I am, but I could not, and now father is dead and Charlie, and mother wants to go home to live with her father, and I am coming home to you! Mother told me to write and ask if I may, and I am very well and happy, but, oh, I am longing to see you and granny. I nearly broke my heart at first, but I am coming home again, and I am so happy, only I am sorry, too, to leave here, and the lady who has been so kind to me. She is old and feels very miserable at being left all alone. Good-bye, granp and granny. I shall come as soon as ever I can when I hear from you. Please write soon. Give my love to granny, I hope she'll soon get better,

> "From your loving,"
> "Jessie Lang."

It was well that Miss Grace stayed by the old couple, for they both needed her by the time the letter was read.

"She is well, and she must have met with kindness, or she would not be sorry to leave," she said cheerfully. "Now, Mrs. Dawson, we shall have her back with us almost at once, so it behoves us to set about getting everything ready for her," she went on, in her sensible, matter-of-fact way, for she felt that the best thing for both of them was to keep them busy with preparations.

Patience caught her spirit at once. "You must write to-night, Thomas," she said eagerly, "you mustn't delay, for the child is waiting for a word and she mustn't be disappointed, whatever happens. I expect she's pretty nigh broken her heart many a time longing to write to us, and—and—her father wouldn't let her. I can read between the lines. I'm sure 'twas his doings—"

"He is dead now," said Miss Grace softly, "so we will forgive him and put away all hard thoughts of him, and maybe your little flower was taken from you just to brighten a dark corner for the time, and bring happiness to others—perhaps to learn some lesson that will help her in the future."

"Maybe," said Patience, but more gently; "my little blossom," she added softly. "P'raps it was greedy to want to keep her to ourselves always."

Thomas had dropped into a chair by the door. "I've got to write, and I can't," he said solemnly, looking up with a half comic, half wistful look in his blue eyes. "My hands is shaking, and my wits is shaking, and—and—but I must, of course, and I am going to Norton to-night to post it, so as the child can get it in the morning."

"No—excuse me—you are not," said Miss Grace, shaking her head at him, laughing, but decisive. "I have my bicycle. I can go there and back in next to no time. With shaking wits and hands you are not fit! Besides, what would Mrs. Dawson do all the evening without you? No, Mr. Dawson, you write the letter and I will do the rest."

She put paper and pens and ink before him on a little table out in the porch, and she and Patience kept very quiet so that they might not interrupt him; but it was no good, he could not write, he really was too much excited and overcome. So at last Miss Grace wrote a little letter for him, one that brought satisfaction to both of them. It expressed their amazement, their joy and excitement, and sent their dearest love, and some little news of them. "Your granny is stronger and more active than she has been for a long time," she wrote, "and perhaps your coming will make her quite well and able to get about again." She felt she ought to prepare Jessie for some of the change she would see.

"There, that is the business part, as you might call it," she said, placing the letter in an envelope, "but I am sure she will worry if there isn't a word from you, Mr. Dawson. Can you write just a tiny message to slip in with mine?—just to say how glad you are."

"Glad!" cried Thomas; "glad is a poor kind of word for what I feel!" He had recovered a little, and was as gay as a schoolboy just getting ready for the holidays. He pulled a piece of paper towards him, and squaring his elbows, he wrote in large round hand:

"Come home quick to granp, and I'll be there to meet you—same as before."
"Your loving grandfather,"
"T. Dawson."

"I haven't wrote a letter before for nigh 'pon twenty years, I b'lieve," he gasped, mopping his brow and stretching his arms with relief, "and now 'tisn't much of a one. I'm out of practice, but the little maid'll understand," and he chuckled happily as he handed it to Miss Grace. "Yes, she'll understand."

Jessie did understand. When the two letters reached her she danced about the house with glad excitement, then flew to Miss Patch to tell her all about them, and about that first meeting with granp at Springbrook station.

Miss Patch listened and sympathized, and rejoiced, too, and in her calm, sweet old face she showed none of the pain which was filling her own poor heart. She was losing every one she cared for, not finding them. All the little daily habits, and pleasures, and friendlinesses, the trifles that made her life, were being taken from her. In a few days more she would be a stranger among strangers, with no one interested enough to care what became of her, and nothing but her room and her flowers would remain the same. And even for how long that much would be left her she could not know.

She would have the same room still, for Mrs. Lang had handed over the house and everything in it, including the lodgers, to some people who wanted a small lodging-house of the kind; but who they were, or what they would be like, was all unknown to Miss Patch.

If, though, she did not show her own feelings then, Jessie found them out a little later. Going unexpectedly up to Miss Patch's room to present her with a geranium which had been one of her own particular treasures, given her by Tom Salter, she found the poor old head bowed on the table, and the poor thin body shaking with sobs. Jessie, in great distress, dropped her geranium and ran to her.

"What is it? What has happened?" she cried. "Oh, Miss Patch, do tell me," and throwing her warm little arms about her old friend, she began to sob, too.

But Miss Patch's self-control had given way at last, and recover herself she could not. Jessie tried to soothe and coax her, but without effect, and she stood beside her at last hopeless, helpless. Her brain was busy, though, and presently light came to her.

"Miss Patch," she said softly, "is it because we are all going away— and you will be left here alone?" Her own voice quavered at the thought.

One of Miss Patch's arms crept round Jessie and drew her close in an almost convulsive grasp. "Yes," she whispered in a choked voice, "I can't—I can't face it—the loneliness it—it—"

A sudden beautiful idea came to Jessie. "Don't stay!" she cried impulsively, without a thought as to ways, or means, or any of the other practical points, "come home with me, come to Springbrook," she cried excitedly. "Oh, do, do, Miss Patch, do. I want you to see granp and granny, and I want them to know you, and—and, oh, it's *lovely* there, and you wouldn't be lonely, you'd have me and granp and granny; and—and it wouldn't cost more, I am sure," she added practically, "it is ever such a cheap place to live in; and—and we would find you a nice room, and, oh, the flowers you'd have—" She had to stop at last from sheer want of breath. But by the time she had done Miss Patch had checked her tears and raised her head, and was staring at Jessie with wide, bright, half-frightened eyes, her face flushed and excited.

"I—it—oh no, it can't be; but—but, oh, how heavenly it sounds to a lonely body like me!" she gasped.

"But it *can* be," cried eager Jessie. "I am sure it can, and it would be lovelier even than it sounds."

"But how could I manage?" gasped Miss Patch, looking dejected again. "Think of my lameness—and there's my furniture."

Jessie looked about her. "There isn't *very* much of it," she said thoughtfully. "I am sure it isn't enough to stop your coming." And she was right, for, after all, there was but the old-fashioned bed and chest of drawers, a chair or two and a couple of tables, and a few boxes and other trifles. "Would you go if your things got there without any trouble—I mean, without any more trouble than changing houses would be? You see," she added wisely, "if you don't like the new people who are coming, you may *have* to change, after all, and then you won't have any one to help you."

The look of dread came back into poor Miss Patch's tired eyes. So gloomy a prospect determined her.

"You are right!" she gasped; "it would be terrible—yes. I'll go—I do believe I will. Oh, my! it's a dreadfully big undertaking, but— but I'll go, yes, I will. I will make up my mind; and—and I won't go back from it. I am terribly given to being a coward, Jessie."

Her mind once made up Miss Patch did not swerve again, and from that time her face grew brighter. And after all it was not such a very big undertaking—not nearly as bad as she had feared, for everything seemed to fall out for her in a perfectly marvellous way, and most of her troubles were taken off her shoulders before she had been able to realize them.

A few letters passed between Jessie and Miss Grace, and then between Mrs. Lang and Miss Grace, and then all seemed to come about so smoothly and easily that Miss Patch scarcely realized all that was being accomplished. Mrs. Lang insisted on paying the charges for the furniture being carried to Springbrook. Tom Salter saw to the packing of them all and sending them off by train; and then, oddly enough, Miss Grace Barley found that she had business in London, and would be returning to Springbrook on the very day Jessie and Miss Patch were expected there, and would travel down with them.

So, on the morning of that day, a cab drove up to the dingy house in Fort Street, and Miss Patch, and her eight parcels, and her rosebush was conveyed to the station in state and comfort, and between Jessie and Miss Grace and Tom she was taken to the railway carriage and comfortably ensconced in a corner without any bother as to luggage or ticket-taking or anything.

In fact, she was so excited and bewildered that she quite forgot all about everything. "Well!" she exclaimed, as the train moved off into the strange new country, "I never knew before how delightful and easy travelling could be! It makes me smile now to think how I shrank from it, and the fuss I made!"

Jessie, who was still weeping silently after the parting with her mother and Tom Salter, looked up and smiled sympathetically. The bustle and responsibility of taking care of Miss Patch had helped them all through the last sad leave-takings, but when that strain was over, and they were comfortably settled, and Tom came up to say his last shy good-bye, the realization rushed over her that she should never see the dingy grey house again, nor her stepmother, nor Tom— good, kind, faithful Tom—and it was with tears running down her face that she threw her arms round the good fellow's neck, and kissed him as though he were her own kind big brother. Then, subsiding into her corner sobbing, she left London in grief nearly as great as when she had arrived there two years before.

For a long time her thoughts lingered about the home and the life she was leaving, her mother, Charlie, her father, the house, the lodgers, the dingy street, the noise and bustle. How real it all seemed, yet already how far away! Could she ever have been in the midst of it with no thought of ever knowing anything else! How strange life was, and how wonderful! How one short month had changed everything! Here she was, her dream and her longing realized, going home again to Springbrook, to the old happy life, the same friends, the same everything—yet, no, not quite the same, never quite the same, perhaps. She herself was changed, and—she looked at Miss Patch. Their eyes met in a happy, affectionate smile. "No, things were not quite the same, they were better, if anything. She had more now, more in every way."

The train tore on, and the day wore on. The hedges were growing bare now, and the leaves on them were turning red and yellow and brown; but the autumn sun shone, and there were space and air and sunshine all about them. Oh, what a change after the close, narrow streets, the gloom and dinginess, the want of space! Jessie's spirits began to rise. How could she be unhappy in this beautiful world, with home before her, and granp and granny waiting for her, and the cottage, and her own dear little bedroom. "Will my rose be alive, do you think, Miss Grace?" she asked eagerly.

"Yes, dear, your grandfather has cared for it as though it were his most treasured possession, and your little garden, too. He has kept everything as though you might return at any moment, and all must be in readiness. It has been a cruelly long parting for them, and it has told on them," she added. "You must be prepared to find them altered. But," she added more cheerfully, "it rests with you to make them young and happy again, Jessie."

"I will do my very, very best," said Jessie earnestly. "Oh!" she sighed, "how slowly the train goes, aren't we nearly there, Miss Grace?"

"Only a few moments now, dear. This is Crossley, the next station to ours. Don't you recognize any landmarks yet?"

Jessie sprang to the window and remained there, fascinated, enchanted, drinking it all in, trying to realize that all was not a happy dream, but glorious reality. She recognized it all now, and every yard made it more familiar.

The train gave a warning whistle. "Here we are! here we are!" she screamed in a perfect ecstasy of joy. "Oh, Miss Grace, there is the road, and—and here is the platform, and—and I do believe I see granp!"

She drew in her head and shrank back into her corner. "Miss Grace," she pleaded excitedly, "when we stop will you and Miss Patch get out and walk away as if I wasn't here and you had forgotten all about me, and then granp will come to look for me—like he did the first time, will you?"

Her eagerness was so great Miss Grace could not refuse her. "Very well, dear, but"—laughingly—"I must leave all the parcels, too. I can't manage them as well."

"Oh, no, we will bring those. Now," as the train drew up, "please get out!"

She drew forward the curtain and hid behind it. Miss Barley and Miss Patch clambered out and walked away. Half-way down the platform they met Mr. Dawson, he was pale and trembling, but his blue eyes, bright with eagerness, looked for one face and figure only, and saw no other; Miss Patch and Miss Barley passed him quite unobserved; Miss Grace smiled to herself, and they turned to watch.

Along the platform he went, peering eagerly into every carriage. Jessie, in her corner, breathless with excitement, thought he would never come. The time seemed so long, so very long, she began to fear that the train would move on and carry her with it. In her excitement she thrust back the curtain, and leaned forward—and the next minute she was in his arms!

"Not asleep this time, granp!" she cried excitedly, "not asleep this time! Oh, granp! granp!" and she hugged and kissed him again and again.

The guard came in at last, to warn them that the train was about to move, and then there was a hasty gathering up of Miss Patch's eight parcels and her rose, and Jessie's three parcels and her geranium, and at last they all stood together on Springbrook platform, with the sun shining on them, the breeze blowing, the birds singing—and granny at home waiting to welcome them to the new happy life which lay before them.

Miss Grace led Miss Patch out, and they got into a carriage which had been sent from Norton for the purpose, but Jessie and her grandfather begged to walk back, as on that first occasion. He did not carry her now, though he leaned on her instead, and seemed glad of the support. He leaned heavily, too, she noticed, and she realized vaguely that there was one more change than she had thought of. In the past she had leaned all her weight on him, now it was he who would lean on her; and she hoped, with all the strength of her warm little heart, that she might be able to prove herself a real prop and staff to him and the dear granny who loved her so.

> "God make my life a little staff,
> Whereon the weak may rest."

She repeated to herself.

"Here's granny," said granp joyfully, as they reached the garden gate. Run on to her, child! and—and remember—one arm is helpless still. You must be her right arm now, Jessie."

"I will," said Jessie eagerly, and the next moment was at her granny's side.3